# SELF-DEFENSE

The open door invited me through it so I darted on into the yard. He lumbered out behind me, bellowing curses at a fearful level of noise and fury.

It was then that I remembered the loosened cinch on my saddle. There was no earthly way I could have tightened it and dashed away before he could reach me. And while he might be slow he looked also to be very powerful. From the way he was shouting now and the darkening of his face I began to be afraid of what would happen if he managed to catch me.

You will understand, then, that it was a matter of justifiable self-defense for me to protect myself. I did no more than I had to do under the circumstances. I pulled the revolver from my waistband and shot the man several times in the chest.

# JASON EVERS:
# HIS OWN STORY

## FRANK RODERUS

LEISURE BOOKS     **L**     NEW YORK CITY

*For my parents, with love and thanks.*

A LEISURE BOOK®

August 1999

Published by

Dorchester Publishing Co., Inc.
276 Fifth Avenue
New York, NY 10001

ISBN 0-8439-4573-7

# JASON EVERS:

# HIS OWN STORY

# Prologue

The other day some sonuvabitch from an Eastern newspaper—I do not remember which one, but then they are all alike anyway—offered me fifty dollars for my life story. A mere fifty dollars, if you can imagine that. I should have thrown him out on the spot, but I was in a reasonably good humor at the time and was already seated with some of the boys from the town, reminiscing with them, and did not see any harm in the newspaperman sitting quiet on the edge of the conversation with his ears open, and that is exactly what I told him he could do.

What the pipsqueak little son did instead was to begin correcting me when I began talking about the shoot-up with McComb and his crowd of hired assassins down on the Arkansas near what is left of old Bent's Fort. You have heard about that one, I know. Everyone has. The thing is, he had heard about it too, and he set in to telling *me* what happened that day, me who was the target of those would-be murderers and who was the one who stood alone to face them. What a bunch of bull he had been told. Not only that, but he *insisted* he was right about it all.

Naturally I became angry—which does happen at times, I must confess—and I became quite adamant about insisting that he leave, which he did hurriedly and in some discomfort. The other boys seemed to get something of a kick out of his departure, and I gave them the fifty dollars this reporter had left behind. With it we set ourselves up to a carry-in feast of roasted prairie hen and half a dozen bottles of a flavorful burgundy, all of which we enjoyed to the fullest.

As I have indicated, it was an amusing incident for those who observed it and one with a pleasant aftermath, but after the departure of my guests I began to reflect on what the pipsqueak had said. And I must believe that he fully accepted the supposed truth of what he had to say about the McComb shoot-up and no doubt about other false tales as well. I do not believe that a puny, chinless, round-hatted ninny like that would intentionally vex Jason Evers. And that knowledge has come to bother me.

I therefore have resolved to set down the whole and complete truth about that and other matters personally observed by me during my lifetime.

Such a record would be without value if I permitted myself to be less than bluntly, ruthlessly honest in every detail. I intend therefore to pull no punches whatsoever. I shall name names and where necessary shall expose even those in high office to full, public knowledge of their misdemeanors and felonies. As did Caesar, they cast their own die. Let them now live under the weight of Truth.

—Jason Evers

# CHAPTER 1

I was born the twenty-ninth day of October in the year 1849, in Brazos County, Texas, the second-born son of Jason Herman Evers and Henrietta Fredrickson Evers. I was christened Jason Randolph Evers, Jason Herman Evers III having died in infancy the winter prior to my birth. Three sisters would follow me into this life, but only one of them would survive into maturity.

My father was a sensible and an industrious man, a tiller of the soil and, later, a shopkeeper dealing in implements and hardwares. He had emigrated to Texas from Henderson County, North Carolina, prior to the Texas War of Independence and was a distinguished participant in the battle of San Jacinto. He later took up residence at Washington-on-the-Brazos and, upon marriage, used his military service land scrip to claim four hundred eighty acres on the farmstead that was to be my fondly remembered boyhood home.

When I was eight my family removed to the capital city, where, it was hoped, our residence would facilitate my father's interests in certain legal matters before the courts. That hope was ill-founded, political cronyism and favoritism being what they are, but my father remained unbowed. He established a greengrocery, which failed due to the rural nature of the capital at that time, but persevered to establish a moderately successful business in implements and hardware.

The opening of the War of Southern Independence excited my boyish fervor, but my father, justly piqued by the government's failure to apply justice to his legal matters, declined further military service. My father expired of the flux during the winter of 1863.

Times were particularly difficult during that period, and my mother was unable to continue operation of the family business. She closed the doors, intending to reopen at a more propitious opportunity, but father's entire stock of goods was attached and sold at auction for a pittance by a rent-greedy block owner. Much litigation was to result from this, but again to no avail. As before, law and justice were to remain unrelated.

In her final recourse to provide for our family, my mother turned our small home into an overnight boarding facility for visitors to the capital city. In this manner she sacrificed her own pride and inherent dignity to the welfare of her children. To this good and selfless woman I shall eternally be grateful.

I, in the meantime, was growing apace. By the commencement of the period of Southern Reconstruction—a particularly severe period for Texas and Texans—I had reached my full stature, although only a youth not yet of age for razor and strop.

Destined to be of lesser physical stature than many, I learned in the streets and alleys of the city that speed and daring skill are often substitutes more than adequate for the protection of one's self from the bullies and the braggarts who are of the opinion that greater size equates to superiority. This is not true.

I have already admitted—because I must be no less harshly honest as concerns myself than I propose to be with others—that I am given to anger, most particularly so when I am in the right and would be thwarted by thugs or liars. This trait was no less true in the heat of my youth. I shall now relate for the first time a factual account of the grossly unjust incident which first set me in jeopardy from those murderers who hide behind the skirts of the law and thereby cloak themselves in a false respectability. Again I shall be bluntly truthful, relating even the falsest and most base of the claims and accusations leveled against myself and my own dear mother.

The incident took place in the wagon park behind Shipton's Livery, where I frequently found errands and odd jobs of work to help supplement the family income. I remember quite distinctly that it was on the late afternoon of the fourteenth day of May in the year 1867.

I was sitting on the tongue of an idle freight wagon, enjoying the sunshine and waiting for an opportunity to perform some small service that might earn me a few cents in return. My thoughts were interrupted by two men who arrived at the wagon park on horseback.

Both men were young and handsomely moustached. One wore the uniform of an officer in the State Police, he thus being one of the white men who supervised the roundly hated coloreds of that dishonorable Reconstruction force. The other, who also had a well-fed Yankee look about him, wore a regular business suit under his unbuttoned duster. Like any good Texan of that time, I ignored the men, but I could not but admire the well-muscled, short-backed horses they rode. Like their owners, the horses were well fed and nicely turned out.

Had those two men had the common decency to go quietly on about their business I do not doubt that my lifetime would have been greatly different than the actual occurrences have been. But in fact they did not, and it is on their eternal consciences that my fate must now rest. I often hoped and prayed that their Northern insensitivity and crudeness of conduct would be repaid—and tenfold—in the hereafter. That is yet one of my most fond hopes.

The incident was begun by the Yankee police lieutenant. Instead of passing decently by me, that officer drew rein and dismounted near to me and motioned for his companion to do the same. He affected a smile when he disdainfully tossed to me the free reins of both animals, but I could clearly see on his lips the contempt shown to a common Southern lad by this grand conqueror from the North. This was even clearer when he spoke.

"They could use water, boy," he said, addressing me the way a gentleman might speak to a nigger, "and tie them out of the sun. There will be a half-dime in it for your trouble." As if his Yankee coin was fit substitute for dignity. But he was being no more than like all other Northerners in that regard. Until he spoke again.

His smile turned even more to a hidden sneer as some sort of recognition entered his eyes.

"Say now, I know who you are. You're the kid that lives at the cathouse over on Fourth. Sure." His evil smile became a laugh. "Hell, boy, for you the job's worth a dime, okay?"

I have never been one to let anger paralyze my instincts, and I did not permit it to happen now.

This bitch-whelped spawn of a Yankee churl had dared to insult my own dear mother and by implication therefore all that was good and true in the womanhood of the South. My anger was as thunder in my ears, but as always this rush of hot passion lent clarity to my brain and speed to my hand.

A linch pin of the heaviest iron and more than a foot in length lay on the footboard of the wagon on which I had been seated. Quicker than thought I grabbed it up and swung it against the side of the foul creature's ear. The blow fell with all the power of my fury and the despicable Yankee cur dropped as does a shoat under the butcher's hammer.

The other man shrieked aloud and fell back into the soft dust of the wagon park, although I had done nothing to intimidate him nor to show myself hostile toward him. I had done no more than give proper defense to the honor of my dear mother and to that of all ladies like her.

The loud cry and sudden movement startled the two animals I continued to hold, forgotten, by the reins. The horses reared in their terror and one succeeded in breaking free and bolting away from the scene, escaping up the alley toward the public street.

By the time I had regained control of the remaining animal the fancily dressed carpetbagger had scrambled to his feet. He was disarranged and disheveled by then and apparently his wits were in a similar state of disarray.

Rather than presenting himself at my side with explanations to confirm the rightness of my course, this cowardly rascal showed his true colors by springing after the disappeared horse with shouts of "Murder! Murder!" on his lips.

I, who had done nothing that could be construed as wrongful, was thus falsely accused of the crime of murder. I could hear this man's hysterical shouting as he gained the street, and the rapid buzz of growing consternation there.

A headquarters for the colored police was only blocks away, and I knew full well that I could expect no justice from them. If I expected to escape with my life I should have to flee the capital city until such time as I could return to the apologies of my present accusers. This was apparent on the face of the situation, as was the fact that a penniless lad of seventeen could not hope to long survive detection in unfamiliar territory. I therefore took the only reasonable course open to me. I quickly knelt to remove the purse from the Yankee officer's pocket and mounted the well-made horse that I still held.

I kicked the beast into a hard gallop down the alley away from the hue and cry, and for the first time in my young life went "on the dodge" from the injustice of the law.

# CHAPTER 2

The horse was not only handsome, he was deep-chested and long-winded as well. I made him show me what he had in him that early evening and on into the night, and it was a gracious plenty he had to offer. I ran him hard for only the first few blocks and then pulled him down into a long lope. Before we were done that first dark and lonesome night, the horse and I had covered the better part of fifty miles, yet, although very tired, he was still sound of wind. I do not, of course, know how far he might have been ridden earlier in the day, before he came into my possession.

Consider if you will now the plight of a hapless youth of only seventeen years, wrenched suddenly and without warning away from the familiar pursuits and loving protection of home and family, alone and friendless in this world, most foully accused when he had done nothing to dishonor name or self but only did that which was reasonable and just.

I daresay I would have been wholly justified had I launched myself on a course of vengeance and rampant destruction. The fact is that I did no such thing, and I believe any sensible observer must hold such voluntary restraint greatly to my credit. I vowed to hold myself to a strictly peaceable course of action then and in the future, insofar as those about me permitted such.

When I judged that I had traveled far enough to escape immediate pursuit I reined the sweating horse to a slow walk and let him calm from his heavy labors.

As it was quite dark and the roads were unfamiliar I had

no way to discover the nature of the terrain, and at this hour no farmstead lights were showing. I therefore allowed the horse to choose his own path away from the public roadway to a small copse or grove of trees where I determined to spend the remainder of the night. I had, by the way, traveled northward from the capital city on the theory that most pursuers would assume me to have turned south toward the *brasada* and the international border.

I was awake—and I must confess nervously so—at first light, cramped and chilled through from a night with no bedding other than a thin woolen saddle blanket, but nonetheless healthy and alert. I was also decidedly hungry, it having been a great many hours since dinner the previous noon. It was with this in mind that I decided to investigate the dead police officer's possessions, in search of any foodstuffs he might have been carrying.

Tied behind the cantle of the small and hornless but in truth not uncomfortable military saddle was a mochila-like leather drape with paired saddle pockets or saddlebags on either side. These I had been in too great a hurry to pause to examine the evening before.

The left-hand pocket yielded little. There was an iron hoof pick, which of course I saved against future need, a rust- and grass-stained snaffle bit, which I also replaced in the leather pouch, a pipe and quantity of tobacco, which I discarded as I did not then nor do I now indulge in that noxious habit, also a leather-bound volume of blank pages, the first few dozen of which contained the beginnings of a journal or diary of the carpetbagging officer. This too I preserved against such future needs toward which waste paper might be put to use. I thought that quite appropriate under the circumstances.

It was the right-hand pocket which proved of real value. In that I found two pasteboard cartons, each containing several dozen paper-wrapped powder-and-ball cartridges, a tin of percussion caps and—most important—a revolver.

The handgun was a military issue Colt's revolving pistol of the popular 1860 Army model. Although it was heavy and somewhat large for my hand, the smoothly flowing lines of the weapon pleased my eye and the balance and excellently formed grip were comfortable to me. It was fully loaded and was capped on five of the six nipples. The chamber under the hammer was uncapped, I supposed for reasons of safety in carrying. At that time I knew little of handguns.

Still, the feel of the weapon in my hand gave me much pleasure, and the knowledge of its power lent me assurance that I would not be lightly taken by those who had so foully betrayed me. Having no holster in which to carry the piece under the secure protection of leather and flap, I shoved the long barrel beneath my waistband against my still empty belly and thus, by that accidental lack of proper equipment, innocently began the trait that would become associated with me to the point of legend. Had it not been for that lack of a slow and restrictive holster, however, I might not now be alive to relate the true events of my life.

Soon thereafter, and still most ravenously hungry, I saddled my horse and made my way back to the public road. As before I chose a north-leading path, wanting as great a distance as possible between myself and any pursuers. There was at this time some twenty-seven dollars of hard money in my purse. Even under those strained circumstances I had the presence of mind to note that my Yankee policeman friend had been carrying hard coin on his person, while those poor unfortunates under his authority were required to accept and pass the worthless governmental scrip of the time. But I digress.

The powerful insistence of my stomach required me to approach the first farmhouse I espied on that bright but cheerless morning. The farmstead was a well-established one, showing signs of prosperous growth over a number of years past. The house was well weathered and had been added onto several times since the original cabin was constructed. In many ways it reminded me strongly of my own boyhood home and of the family that was now lost to me. Perhaps because of this superficial resemblance and my resulting emotional state of mind, my wariness and innate sense of caution were not what they should have been when I first saw the hardheaded Dutchman who farmed these acres.

I found him at work in his barn, bent over some moldering scraps of leather harness that should have been thrown away but which he seemed to be trying to patch together into a usable whole. He gave the appearance of being a typical squarehead farmer, burly and unclean, but closely shaven and nearly as closely cropped atop his skull as along his jowls. His skin was dark and deeply lined, his clothing ragged and much patched. His greeting at first seemed a pleasant one.

He spoke a civil welcome and said, "You like to missed finding me at home, boy, except this damned breeching strap slowed my morning work. Is there anything I can do for you?"

"I haven't eaten since early yesterday, mister. Could you or your missus fix me a breakfast and maybe a poke to carry with me?"

Immediately the man's welcome turned to brisk and greedy business. I could see it in his eyes as plain as pitch. He nodded. "Get a lot of travelers here, we do. Every week it seems like. Twenty-five cents the breakfast. That again for the poke. All right?"

It seemed a robber's price, as I could have gotten a proper meal in town for that, and I was somewhat angered, but I had no choice. "Done," I told him.

"Real money," he said. "No paper." He was pushing at me even further—and needlessly as I had no money but coin— but again I had no choice.

"Twice twenty-five," I agreed. "In coin."

He laid his mending aside and stood, and I could see then that he was a great, tall fellow, as well as a big-built man. "Put your horse in the pen there. Give him hay if you want."

"And the charge?" I asked with my chin shoved forward.

"No charge for dumb animals," he said.

I stepped down from the good horse and loosened the girth, although I had foresight enough in my flight to leave him saddled. I put him into the small, cedar-post pen the man had indicated. There was already a hay-filled crib in a corner of the enclosure, and the stout bay horse moved to it. I, the meanwhile, followed my host.

The man led across the farmyard to the cool, dim interior of the log-walled oldest portion of the house. It was fronted with a covered veranda or porch and on either side were newer wings made of sawed timbers. The oldest logs had not even been squared.

"My old woman's away," the man said over his shoulder as we entered the kitchen, "but she's no better a cook than me anyway. Set while I fix something."

I waited at the table, a finely crafted piece of furniture carried in from elsewhere and not the rudely home-built job one might have expected, while he rebuilt the fire in his stove and set on a generous amount of plain fare to heat. He also poured coffee, which was still warm if not hot, but was bitter with age. I told him I hoped the food was better than the coffee.

"You can still change your mind," he told me. The insolence was heavy in his voice. "If you don't wanta eat just say so."

I had no choice in the matter or I might have gone elsewhere for my meal. As it was I controlled my impulse for retort and said nothing.

When finally it came the food was at least as poor as the coffee and I could not help but mutter so, although under my breath and therefore not rudely. It was not at all my intention to vex the man, you see, but only to partially relieve myself of the burden of discomfort he had placed on me through no fault of my own.

He for some reason took offense to my honest complaint and said, "Listen, boy, this ain't a roadhouse and it's only by my good nature that you got anything to eat at all. Now you can just damn well learn to mind your manners and not be complaining about my good wife's food, you hear?"

His tone was ugly and belligerent, I thought, and that pleased me no better than the meal had. It was only natural that I should return heat for heat in my answer.

"By God, old man, you just listen yourself then. My ma wouldn't have fed this slop to a hog, and that's a fact. What's more, if it was your good nature that gave me this meal and not the promise of twenty-five cents hard money, then I will by damn keep my money and tell you to go to hell."

On that note I arose from his fine table and clapped my old hat firmly onto my head.

"You little . . ." I don't know what else he intended to say, for he started at the same moment to lunge toward me with the anger drawing his face into a grimace.

He was an old man, though, and slow. I was laughing as I ducked under his rush.

The open door invited me through it, so I darted on into the yard. He lumbered out behind me, bellowing curses at a fearful level of noise and fury.

It was then that I remembered the loosened cinch on my saddle. There was no earthly way I could have tightened it and dashed away before he could reach me. And while he might be slow, he looked also to be very powerful. From the way he was shouting now and the darkening of his face I began to be afraid of what would happen if he managed to catch me.

You will understand, then, that it was a matter of justifiable self-defense for me to protect myself. I did no more than I had to do under the circumstances. I pulled the revolver from my waistband and shot the man several times in the chest.

It was later said that the man had stopped when I drew my revolver and had the time to beg for his life before I shot him. I do most emphatically deny that my actions were cruel or in any manner base; I acted solely from a sense of self-preservation and would do so again today if confronted with a similar situation.

It should be remembered that these unjust accusations were made by the farmer's widow, who had every reason to lie and none to give me justice. No reason, that is, but simple fairness, and neither she nor her deceased husband seemed so inclined.

I have no way of knowing, of course, whether she was actually in a position to view the events—as she later claimed to have been—but it is undeniable that someone was at or near the scene to give the Laws a reasonably accurate description of me in my hour of desperation, by which means my identity was linked to the death of that farmer Dutchman. Personally I saw no one else at the scene or I might have appealed to them to state the facts properly. As it was I simply reclaimed my horse, tightened his cinch and made my way away from that place.

It should be seen as being to my credit, I should hope, that I made no attempt to take any possessions from the dead farmer nor from his homestead. I left that place fed, it is true, but still without the supply of provisions the man had agreed to prepare for me before he caused our falling out. I could easily have taken whatever I chose from the place, but I did not do so. Instead I made a hasty departure, this time avoiding the public roads in favor of the smaller lanes winding through the rolling, wooded country north of the capital. For I remained at the mercy of the cruel and unfeeling Laws and of those who might choose to report me to them in exchange for thirty pieces of silver or whatever other reward might have been placed on my innocent head.

# CHAPTER 3

That evening I came upon a most remarkable gentleman, an encounter which might have greatly changed my fate had things been only slightly different later. Again it was my much-abused and too-long-empty belly which led to the encounter.

In the last, dim light of the day I saw at some distance before me a firelight and wagon and a shadowy picket line of horses. Being fearfully hungry I set caution aside and approached the camp.

I was both surprised and pleased to discover that the camp was tended by a lone individual, a man in his later years, full of beard and dark of eye, a man but little taller than I and ruggedly built in spite of the white in his beard. He stood and faded back into the shadows at the sound of my arrival.

"Step down and make yourself welcome," he called out in a pleasant enough tone.

By this time I was close enough to realize that the picket line held more animals than a single wagon would require, and I did not know how many men might be around me in the new night. I moved carefully to comply, a sinking sensation burdening my already groaning stomach.

"What is it you want?" the voice came again.

"A meal is all I want," I responded. "I'm alone on the road and very hungry, sir."

I heard what might have been the soft click of a revolver being let off cock and a moment later he stepped back into the light, his hands empty and no holster showing beneath his much-worn coat.

"What's your name, boy?"

"Ja . . . ," I started. "Jay Evans, sir. Of Washington-on-the-Brazos."

"You have a lot to learn, boy," he said mildly. He squatted beside his fire and jiggled a three-legged pot resting on the coals beside the flame. "You should be better prepared than that. Use a different sound entirely. Something like . . . oh . . . Duncan." He smiled. "Yes, I think I like that. Duncan Reeves. Jay Evans is entirely too close to Jason Evers, you see. The next time someone asks, tell them you're Duncan Reeves." He put a hand forward. "I'm Jonathon Keene, Duncan."

Stupidly, much shocked by his words, I accepted his handshake. Jonathon Keene smiled sadly and shook his head.

"Another mistake, Duncan. Never shake hands with a man who knows who you are. I could keep your hand away from that gun in your belt and box your ears for you." He released my hand and reached to jiggle the pot again. "You see what I mean?"

"But . . . ?"

"How? Simple. I heard talk about you at two different crossroads settlements today. Very different stories. I try not to judge until I know. You can tell me your side of it while we eat, Duncan."

So I did, between mouthfuls from the plate he provided, relating my sorry tale much as I have already set it down here, leaving out only the events of the morning.

When I was done Jonathon Keene fixed a stare on me that was so penetrating I was sure it could reach to my bones and search out all the secret, small embarrassments of my entire past. It was not a comfortable feeling and I daresay I may have squirmed a little under his inspection.

After what seemed a long time he said, "There are things

you haven't told me, Duncan, but I believe there is good in you yet. If you want to pursue that good and put the bad behind you, you may come with me as my helper."

"Why?" I could not help asking.

His answering smile was distant, as with old memories fondly retained. "Call it repayment of a debt if you like." And that was all he ever told me on that subject.

In many, many ways I suppose I should have been reluctant to accept such unexpected help from a man I had never seen before, but once again circumstance had left me with little real choice open before me. If my description and name were known already so accurately and so widely, it seemed only sensible to let Duncan Reeves replace Jason Evers on the road ahead. I still did not know if I could trust this man and in truth trusted him very little then, but here was at least a chance and I had to take it. Besides, Jonathon Keene had already taught me several things that might prove useful in the future. If he could teach me more I would be only foolish to reject the opportunity.

"You have a new helper, Mr. Keene," I told him. Remembering his own advice, I did not offer to shake on the bargain just made.

Jonathon Keene, it transpired, was a traveling man of several talents and numerous occupations. His light wagon held a collection of small tools with which he could work both wood and metal. He had a grindstone with which to sharpen anything from scythes to scissors. He maintained a small stock of needles and colored threads and other small bits he might be able to sell to those far removed from stores. At the tailgate of the wagon usually trailed a string of horses or mules available for sale or trade. He followed no schedule or set route but wandered wherever the roads took him, slept wherever darkness found him, performed whatever tasks would pay. He seemed content.

In the morning he had me scatter his livestock onto fresh grass—a four-up of good mules on the wagon, a rough

drafter and several light saddle horses in the trade string—
and told me we would not move on this day.

I was apprehensive about this, thinking still in terms of
flight, but he said, "Tomorrow there will be no such person
as Jason Evers, and as soon as a new brand has healed there
will be no government horse to be found either."

"All right then," I agreed reluctantly. I was glad that I
did.

Jon Keene was an artist with a pair of smith's tongs and
fire-heated scraps of old metal. The old US brand on my
horse became an O5 Bar, each new stroke the same width
and depth as the years-old government brand. He put a
salve over the new burns and said that in the morning he
would stain the wounds dark enough to pass casual inspection. To further hide the identity of the animal a dye oblit-
erated a white snip on the horse's muzzle, and its handsome
tail was clipped raggedly short.

My own sandy-colored hair was also washed with a dark
dye, and Keene had me exchange my clothing for some
cast-off garments from his wagon. The transformation, he
said, would not fool anyone who had known Jason Evers,
but would be more than ample for those who would meet
Duncan Reeves.

The .44 Army he absolutely insisted I should keep out of
sight. On this point I argued, and in the end we reached a
compromise. He agreed to show me some tricks on how to
bring the big gun into play quickly if I would agree to bring
it out of hiding and practice with it only when he judged it
safe to do so. For protection at other times he let me carry
in a pocket a .32 rimfire Smith and Wesson of the type so
popular during the war because of the new-style contained
cartridges. This I agreed to, although I had much less
confidence in the little gun than in the big .44.

Again, however, this proved to be a stroke of fortune, for
he was able to show me how to cock my revolver as I was in
the act of pulling it rather than first pulling, then cocking,

then aiming as is generally considered normal. After a time I learned to be quite quick at bringing a cocked revolver from my waistband and lining it up onto the target as it came out. As I was naturally quick with my hands I readily became adept at this.

Jonathon Keene also dealt a bit in books, and when he learned that I could read but poorly he insisted that I practice reading an hour each evening before I should be permitted to practice with the pistol.

"Jason Evers was an uneducated youth," he said, "but Duncan Reeves is going to be exposed to much better thoughts and keener minds than were available to Evers."

At first I agreed only to humor Keene, but I came to enjoy the exercise and soon looked forward to each trade that might bring a new volume into the wagon in exchange for one already read.

We traveled slowly, often in comfortable silence, and I came to know that Jon Keene was a good man.

# CHAPTER 4

"Never cheat a man. It isn't necessary. If you can't make a profit honestly—and the reason for being in any business is to make a profit—it means you are in the wrong business. Change your business, not your methods. Cheating a customer is bad business. It gives you a bad name. You can put five dollars more in your pocket today but lose fifty dollars next week because the next fellow won't deal with you," was one of the things he told me while we rode down the dusty market roads.

"You don't follow any regular route. The people you trade with never heard of you," I reminded him.

"Don't you believe that, Duncan. People talk. Names and happenings get around. When people get together they will talk about anything they've seen or done or heard since the last time they spoke, anything from their mule colicking to a neighbor girl getting in trouble with a wandering peddler. And you will find that the bigger and the emptier the country you are passing through, the more people will talk whenever they find someone to talk with."

He gave me a hesitant look and added, "If you ever have to hide yourself in the future, you will do it easier in a big city than in the most remote desert or the deepest mountains, Duncan. In a city the people will see a thousand strangers every day and ignore all of them. In empty country an unknown man is seen and discussed and wondered about. In the city people talk about fires or prices or prizefights or such exciting things or amusements. In empty country people will talk about things as trivial as a set of hoofprints left where none had been expected. Remember that."

"I will," I said. And I did.

He smiled. "Not that you need ever have use of that knowledge, Duncan. I want you to remember that too."

"Yes, sir."

He didn't just talk about the way things should be done, though. He did them.

I remember a place we stopped at the first week I was with him. It was about a hundred miles east of where I had met him and not close to any town that I knew of.

The farm was well established and a lot of clearing done, probably fifty acres or more under cultivation. The family's sons were mostly grown, and there was a daughter old enough that her bigger brothers were keeping close track of her.

We drew up in the yard and Jon raised the canvas side of the wagon to show what all he had to offer. The family started trooping out from the house and the field and the sheds.

"We won't get any laboring jobs here," Jon said when he saw the boys, "but we might sell a thing or two."

The women, mother and girl, reached us first and began to admire the things in the wagon. The daughter, who wasn't hardly pretty enough to have to be watched over, was wanting a piece of fancy cloth, but was shut off in no uncertain terms. The mother took two spools of thread and admired but did not buy a new pair of shears.

The father was the last to reach us. He introduced himself as W. T. Ingram and stood back with his arms folded until the rest of his family had done looking. Finally he moved up closer and tilted his head toward the string of animals tied to the tailgate.

"Those are available too, I reckon?"

"They are," Jon agreed.

The man made a sour face. "Guaranteed sound, I suppose?"

In a completely serious voice Jon said, "Mr. Ingram, I don't guarantee them to have four legs apiece. But you're welcome to count them for yourself."

It surprised me, but Ingram seemed quite satisfied with that response. In fact, he began to look a lot more interested than he had been. He walked around to the back of the wagon and began inspecting the heavy animals tied there along with four light saddlers, my horse among them.

"What about that one?" Ingram asked. He pointed to a handsome and very large draft cross that looked like it had a good bit of French blood in it. It was a good-looking horse, no doubt about it, steely gray and with all the muscle in the world.

"It's a horse," Jon agreed.

"Lead him out," Ingram said, recrossing his arms and giving the animal a critical stare.

Jon gave me a nod, so I unclipped the gray from the lead line and stood him up for the farmer. I led the horse to and from him at a walk and at a trot. I held the big animal's head while Ingram examined his mouth and felt of his legs and chest. It was a nice-mannered horse and stood quiet through the whole procedure.

Ingram nodded finally and turned to one of his boys. "Go fetch Lunk for the gentleman to look at," he said.

The boy ran off and pretty soon came back leading a much lighter-built horse that had some harness sores marring its front end. Jon took a cursory look into its mouth and returned his attention to Ingram.

"What do you have in mind?" Jon asked.

The farmer raised one hand to pull at his lip while he thought it over. "My horse and twenty-five," he said finally.

Jon shook his head. "No."

"It's a fair price," Ingram protested. "I'm not a dickering

man, sir. I offered what I thought was fair. Your horse ain't worth more to me."

"Less," Jon said agreeably.

"What?"

"I don't know you, Mr. Ingram. Are you a man who resents the advice of strangers?"

"I am not."

Jon pondered that for a moment. I was coming to know him well enough by then to guess that he was making something of a show about how much he was debating whether he should say more. After a bit he gave an almost imperceptibly small nod and said, "The horse would be worth that or more to a man in town, maybe. There is muscle enough there to move a brick bank building, but his feet are small for all that body. He'll do better with shoes and a firm surface. He'd bog too deep in mud or in plowed soil, for his feet are no larger than your horse's. You can have him if you want him, of course. Trade and twenty would be fair. Or you could have that chestnut at the same price. Your choice."

Ingram eyed first Jon and then the horse. He picked up the near forefoot and laid his palm across it, did the same with his own horse and grunted once. I took that as an admission that Jon had been right. "I'll look at the other," he said.

I led the slightly smaller chestnut out, and we went through the whole inspection process again. Ingram stood the chestnut up beside his horse and compared them. The chestnut was nearly a hand taller and carried much more muscle. "You say he's sound?"

"I said I don't guarantee them. Can you guarantee yours won't lie down and die tomorrow?"

"You know I can't."

"Neither can I."

"Do you know of any unsoundness?" Ingram persisted.

"I do not."

"Trade and twenty, you said?"

Jon nodded.

Ingram pursed his lips, thought for a moment. He turned to his wife. "Go get the man his money, Sarah. Carl, Henry, go put this one in harness. We'll see how he works." To Jon he said, "The little cob has lots of heart, but he's thin-skinned. Galls too easy. I'd say I got the best of it."

"Then we're both happy," Jon said. "He will do just fine on a light wagon, I think. Someone will use him."

Ingram accepted a twenty-dollar gold piece and a slip of paper from his woman and handed both to Jon. Jon rummaged in a folio under the wagon seat for the chestnut's bill of sale and a pencil. Both men signed, and the deal was complete.

"Now do you know of any unsoundness?" Ingram asked.

"Only in the gray," Jon said with a small smile. "But if you count them, I *think* you will find four legs on the chestnut."

Ingram grinned, the first expression of pleasure he had given, and shook Jon's hand. "Stop again the next time you're through here."

"We will."

I put the new horse into our string and we drove away.

"Would you really have sold him the gray for twenty?" I asked when we were out of earshot.

"Uh-huh."

"Do you think you can get more for him elsewhere?"

"If we're lucky. We'll make something off of him anyway. I can't see that it matters when."

"You had less in the chestnut, didn't you?" I asked.

"About the same," he said. He followed it with a sharp look that told me to shut up. He was getting annoyed with me, and I began to wonder if maybe he really didn't have an angle in the deal that I didn't know about. If he had one I couldn't find it.

# CHAPTER 5

Jon Keene's way of living was slow and comfortable and easy to get used to. He never worried about making time or putting any particular number of miles behind us in a day. People who wanted to talk always found that he had the time for them, and we spent more than a few nights in strange beds at places where the people hadn't had enough conversation by nightfall and wanted to take it up again in the morning.

We rambled east that way through the farm country, turned south for a while and then went west again. We never got quite so far as the Gulf of Mexico, which I regretted. I had heard about it, of course, and would have enjoyed the sight of so much water.

After a time we got into country where the drinking water became less and less frequent, and it became even harder to believe there could be one single body of water stretching further than the eye could see.

As the supply of water lessened we made more and more of our stops in places where there were homes or even settlements. We were away from the farms then and into stock-raising country. By then Jon had traded off most of the draft animals in his swap string and was offering rough-looking saddlers instead. These were not worth as much as a drafter, but we led more of them. And anyway Jon never seemed to worry that much about his income.

"There will be enough," he told me once when I asked. "A man couldn't hardly starve in this country unless he really worked at it. Anything beyond that is mere surplus, Duncan."

"Yes, sir," I said. I always tried to be polite with him. Still, it seemed that those with the money always had the best of things, and I don't mean only of those things tangible. My experience in the capital had been that the "haves" necessarily overcome the "have nots," as in the case of my mother and the unfair lease-holder or before that in my father's several court disputes. Given a choice I would much prefer to be a "have." I have no doubt, though, that Jon Keene could have been a much wealthier man than he was, if only he had chosen to pursue wealth with greater diligence.

There apparently were some, however, who believed that Jon was a wealthy man, and in a town called El Paso del Norte I was able to repay some of the gratitude I felt toward him.

As the town was on a main route of commerce our recent sales had been slim, but Jon was able to take advantage of the situation to restock our supplies of minor trade items such as threads and awls and the always popular bits of colored cloth which he loaded now in increased quantity. He paid for our purchases in cash, as horses here seemed to be in plentiful supply.

That evening we chose to drive out away from the town and sleep at the wagon with the stock rather than pay a fee to accommodate them at one of the public yards. As Jon was not a man given to carousing even on those few occasions when the opportunity existed for such, we rolled into our blankets at the usual early hour and left the fire untended.

I was at that time quite over my fear of pursuit and so had resumed my habit of sleeping heavily in the manner of any youth. I was at the time still but seventeen years of age.

At some hour of the night I became groggily aware of the sound of harsh voices near my bed beneath the wagon box.

For a time I had difficulty separating these sounds from those heard in a dream, but as the sounds persisted and the tone of argument deepened I realized that this was no nightmare. I raised my head from the leather saddlebags I used for a pillow and tried to see what was causing this annoying commotion.

Jon's bed, laid as usual near the now-dead fire, was empty, and I could see four shapes in the starlit night. One of them had to be Jon, but I could not be certain which. Nor in my sleep-dulled uncertainty did I immediately think to approach the group. My attention soon sharpened, however.

"I will *not*," Jon's voice came to me in the darkness. His tone was low and controlled, but it held a stubborn anger I had not heard there before.

Someone in the group laughed. "We think you will. Of course it don't make any difference to us. We've tried to be reasonable about this. Just think of it as a kind of toll charge, you see. If you don't want to pay the cash, though, you'll lose it all, friend, and maybe your life besides. You take your pick."

"We know you have cash on you, old man," another voice interjected. "You paid in coin for the things you bought in town today. We just want you to share a little stake with us."

The laughter rang out again. "You'll get it back, of course."

"You do trust us, don't you?"

"It'd be damned insulting if you didn't trust us."

"So you really oughta be neighborly when we are in need and you ain't."

"I already told you," Jon said stubbornly. "I will not be a participant in the robbing of my own possessions."

"But this ain't a robbery," one of them insisted. "It's like a toll charge."

"Just the loan of a stake, from a rich man to some poor ole boys in need of what you have."

"It is extortion of the grossest kind, and when you boys sober up tomorrow you will be ashamed of yourselves. Unless I give in to you. Then you would be robbers. As it is you can still leave my camp with no worse than a shameful memory. I suggest you do that before you ruin your lives with an act you will regret later." There was a strong sound of finality in Jon's tone.

Apparently the footpads—for they were no better than that—could hear that also, for one of them stepped away from the group and pulled a revolver from the holster at his belt. For the first time I was able to identify for certain which of the figures was Jon.

"We need the stake, mister. We intend to have it."

I did not doubt that their intent was murderous, and by this time the fog of sleep was fully cleared from my brain.

My first inclination was to reach into my saddlebags for the big .44 I carried there, but I remembered in time that that weapon was uncapped, as I had been practicing a rapid draw and Jon always insisted that I do so with the utmost safety. I did have the little .32 rimfire in my coat pocket beside my bed, though, so it was this that I took up. The sound of it being drawn to cock apparently went unheard by the men who surrounded Jon.

He, however, seemed to be aware of it, for even in the darkness I could see a stiffening of his frame when the thin, metallic click sounded in the cool air.

"Turn and leave now, boys, while you still have the chance. Before you wind up hurt," he said quickly.

"Before *we* get hurt? The hell you say." The one with the pistol in his hand raised it to point toward Jon, and I touched off the .32.

For such a small dog the little gun had a loud yap, and the noise reverberating down off the wagon box floor fairly deafened me. The powder flash was terribly bright as well, and for a moment I was blinded by the brief glare.

By the time I could see again Jon was flat on the ground and the three would-be robbers were in panicked flight. I scrambled out from under the wagon and emptied the little revolver in the direction they had run. I ran then to Jon's side.

"I'm fine," he said calmly. He got to his feet and brushed the dirt from his trousers.

"They all got away," I said.

"That's all right. They won't be back." He sighed. "They were just liquored up. I could smell it all over them. The scare will sober them fast enough. I just hope that one boy wasn't hurt too badly."

"I hit him then?"

"Yes, I'm afraid you did. I suppose it was necessary under the circumstances."

I felt considerably better after hearing that, although I never did learn how badly the man was wounded or whether he died from the bullet. "You are all right now?" I asked.

"Quite," he assured me.

After daybreak I made a search of the area nearby, but could find no bloodstains or other evidence that my shots had taken effect. I resolved thereafter to keep the .44 Army loaded and capped except when I was actually engaged in practice with it. I have done so ever since.

# CHAPTER 6

The stage road ran westward through the dry, rough country from El Paso del Norte, and another went north and south, down into Old Mexico or up toward Santa Fe. None of this country was heavily populated. It was also poorly watered, one fact presumably explaining the other. As our business was better served when we were off the more heavily traveled roads, Jon turned the team north into New Mexico.

That first evening he reminded me that Texas was now behind me.

Perhaps, considering the unfair but nevertheless lawful charges I had left behind me, I should have drawn a breath of relief at the knowledge that I no longer was on Texas soil, but in fact what I felt was a great welling of homesickness. This was the first time in all my young life that I had been out of the state of my birth and, while it may seem somewhat odd, it was this departure and not my abrupt leave-taking from home that prompted within me an empty sense of loneliness.

I believe Jon was somehow aware of what I felt, for that night he talked to me of the far places he had been and of some of the wondrous things he had seen. Vast plains covered with grass and wildflowers and buffalo, high mountains so tall the passes remained filled with snow into June or later, rugged canyons carved out of red rock that took shapes only the devil could have conceived, and an ocean so large the men who sailed on it had to stay on its waters for months or even years at a time.

Had I not already been caught up in the pleasures of reading I doubt that I would have believed the tenth part of what he said, but as it was his sense of adventure soon commanded my attention and pushed the loneliness from my mind.

The next day it was back to business as usual, though, and in the days that followed we drove north and west, following the lesser roads and again avoiding the highway. We traded a few horses and acquired a short string of mules in their place. We helped a lone rancher dig a well that came in sweet and clear and on the strength of that success tried to do the same for his neighbor seven miles distant, but that effort ended in failure. Jon gave me a portion of the funds we earned from our labor. I accepted the wage even though it was paid in paper.

Jon also judged that the brand on my good bay horse was sufficiently healed that it would pass inspection. He suggested that we trade the animal at the earliest opportunity.

"I don't want to do that," I told him stubbornly. "He is by far the finest horse I have ever had. I don't want to give him up."

"He is a fancy horse, Duncan," Jon agreed, "but he is entirely too fine to keep."

"That doesn't make sense," I insisted.

"Not at all so," he said. "A horse of that quality catches a man's eye and remains in his memory. Anyone seeing you on him will remember you, because of him. You should think about that. The choice is yours, of course, but I would suggest you let me trade him for you, for a horse with as much wind and as much heart but with less fine an appearance. Something people will not remember once it has passed and gone.

"I doubt you could find another as good."

Jon shrugged. "If I cannot there will be no trade then. The question is whether I should make the deal if I find a horse as good or better. And whether you will accept my judgment if I do."

I looked again at the beautifully formed bay and was sure that Jon Keene could not possibly find his equal. On the other hand I was by then willing to believe that if Jon Keene told me another horse was better, why then it was better even if to me it looked like an underweight burro fit only for the carrying of pots and pans. And what he had said about leaving no strong impressions was only sensible. "I will accept your judgment on the matter," I told him.

Although he would never admit to it—and I did ask several times—I am sure in my own mind that Jon knew somehow what we would find at the next ranch we came to. It is undeniable that he had previously known the man who lived there.

We pulled into the yard just short of midday and a tall, gray-haired man with a makeshift cane hobbled onto the veranda of the adobe-walled house.

"Keene? By God, it is. I'd recognize that rig anywhere."

The two men shook hands and Jon motioned toward the cane and the man's game leg. "Have you gotten old since I saw you last, Charlie?"

The man named Charlie took no offense at the question, but threw his head back and laughed. "It's been 'most long enough, hasn't it. What is it now, five years? Six?"

"Something like that."

"It must be. I was still on the old place then, back in Texas still it was. I never thought to see you here, by God."

"Well, you know how I am about wandering. And it is good to see you again. How's Jessica?"

"You didn't hear then, Keene. She died not long after I started this place. Took her home for burying when I went back for the last herd."

"I'm sorry to hear that, Charlie."

Charlie shrugged. "It's part of living. I married a Mex'can

woman, oh, 'bout four years ago now. She cooks good. Keeps me warm at night."

"If you're still thinking about that I guess you aren't so old yet."

Again Charlie laughed. "Not yet, Keene. Not that old." He slapped a heavy hand onto the thigh of his game leg, hard enough that it was like he was punishing the leg more than indicating it. "This damn thing is from a fall. Can you believe it? Man my age oughta know better, but I hooked a spur in my own rigging and the horse came down with me still astraddle of him. Fool thing to do, it was."

"Like you said, Charlie. It's part of living."

"I suppose. Listen though, Keene, we're standing out here in the yard like a couple strangers an' I don't even have a hat on. Let's go inside and get comfortable."

Jon nodded. "Duncan, unhitch everything and water them, would you? Come inside when you're done."

"Yes, sir."

"You can turn them all into that pen yonder," Charlie said. "We won't start dinner without you."

I did as I was told and when I got inside both Jon and his friend were settled in heavy armchairs with their feet propped up and mugs of dark home brew at their elbows.

They seemed to be talking about places and people I didn't know of, so I took a seat kind of off to the side and admired the room.

The house was a big place, much bigger even than it looked from the outside. The walls were thick and the many windows and doors were roof-shaded so that it was cool inside, with plenty of air flow to keep it even nicer.

The furniture was heavy, but each piece was given plenty of room between it and the next one so it didn't look crowded. The floor was made of tiles and had some small rugs scattered here and there with bright colors. Other rugs with designs woven into them had been hung on the walls. There were enough lamps and candlesticks scattered around to make the whole place day-bright if they were all lighted at once. There was an air about the place that said that Mr. Charlie was wealthy enough to have things exactly as he wanted them and that this was exactly what he did want. If he had been here only half a dozen years or so he had done a lot of building and fixing in that time, for the place looked well settled into and much older than that.

A Mexican woman served us a huge dinner at a table in another room. She didn't eat with us, so I doubt she was Charlie's wife. The food was mostly Mexican too, spicy but very good. After dinner the men decided to talk a little business.

"Are you dragging anything with you that I can't live without, Keene?"

"Do you need a paper of pins, Charlie? Or some thread? Maybe you have some knives for me to sharpen."

Charlie laughed.

Jon smiled and said, "Surely you don't expect me to believe you let that string of animals walk right by you without you looking them over. What's more, if you weren't interested you wouldn't have brought the subject up."

"No point, I don't s'pose, in starting talk on the other one and switching?"

Jon shook his head. We had only two horses on the string at the time, my bay and a very ordinary pony. The rest were mules.

"In that case we'll get straight to it," Charlie said. "What do you want, cash or trade?"

"Trade."

Charlie nodded. He rang a little bell on the table beside his place and the Mexican woman showed up in the doorway to the kitchen. He told her something in Spanish. To us he said, "There'll be some possibles in the corral in a few minutes."

We each had another cup of coffee and Charlie led the way outside, this time clapping an old hat on.

A bunch of geldings had been run into the pen next to the one where I'd put our animals, and a couple of vaqueros were in there with them, afoot and with big coils of rope in their hands. The men were hazing the horses back and forth in the corral.

"Take your pick," Charlie invited.

Jon smiled. "Straight out or do we want to switch around some?"

Charlie laughed. "Straight out, Keene."

Now I hadn't had time yet myself to count the horses, much less to go through and appraise them one against the other, but apparently Jon Keene had already seen all he needed to. He pointed with his chin toward a far corner of the pen and said, "The yellow back there with the scarred pasterns."

Again Charlie tipped his head back to laugh, and this time he roared. "By God, Keene, I had the boys put them other twenty head in there just to see if you could find him in with them. An' you did it even quicker than I could have." He shook his head and then called out something in Spanish.

One of the Mexicans gave his loop a brief twirl and a flip, and the rope snaked out over the backs of the others to settle on the neck of a horse I could barely see in all that crowd.

The animal that was led out seemed nothing at all special. His coat was a washed-out yellow so pale it looked gray in spots. He was Roman-nosed and heavy-necked. Yet on closer look I could see that his legs were straight and long, his barrel deep and his nostrils wide for gathering in the wind. He didn't look like much until the fourth or fifth inspection, but there was a good bit of horse there. And he had a good, honest look in his eyes.

"He'll do," Jon said.

"Do you want me to bring the bay out?" I offered.

Jon grinned and raised an eyebrow toward his friend.

"Hell no," Charlie said. "I seen him already." You would have thought I had insulted the man by offering to show him my horse. Why, sometimes a farmer will spend half a day feeling of a horse and judging him and still not be able to make up his mind. This old rancher had seen my bay on a lead rope and looked at him so casually I hadn't even noticed him looking at all, yet he seemed convinced he knew all he needed to know about the horse. But then maybe he did at that. "How do you want to trade?" he asked Jon.

"Straight out or dicker?" Jon asked him back.

"Straight out, by God."

"The yellow and seventy-five."

"You're dickering, by God."

Jon shrugged. "Make an offer."

"Sixty."

"Seventy."

Charlie laughed. "Let's jump the last step. Sixty-seven fifty and done."

"Done," Jon said.

"We'll settle up inside." Charlie said something more in Spanish, and the vaquero holding the yellow horse—my yellow horse—led him off to the other pen to make the exchange for the bay horse.

Jon completed the paperwork inside and collected the money, which he turned over to me—all of it, as a matter of fact—when we were alone.

We spent the night there and started fresh in the morning with a big breakfast under our belts and a supply of meat in the wagon that Charlie wouldn't take pay for.

# CHAPTER 7

That damned ugly old yellow horse was everything Jon Keene promised and maybe more. Not that I should really call him old. He was only six, just coming prime. He just looked old. Acted old, too.

In some ways he was the laziest horse I ever came across. He never fidgeted or pawed and seemed to be asleep most of the time, including when he was walking on the lead line. Put a saddle on him and he would wake up enough to twitch an ear maybe, if he was well rested. Get up on his back and he was still as lively as a rock lying in the road.

Pick up the reins, though, and I could tell by his ears that he was alive. Nudge him in the ribs and he would break into a smooth run. Kick him and it was like falling off a cliff. He would stretch it out like no horse I ever saw and the wind would come back into my face and roar across my ears in a way I had never expected to know.

It was a joy to ride him and I began to spend much of my time doing so. I enjoyed running him, too, and he seemed to take to it as much as I did.

I learned quickly enough—the truth is, really, that Jon pointed it out to me—that the yellow was not a sprinter, but a real speedburner once he reached his stride.

"Look at him closely, Duncan, and you can see why. He is long-legged and long-muscled, long and lean in the hindquarters and deeply built in the front."

Jon smiled at me and went on. "Some time soon, Duncan, you will want to race this horse of yours."

I was somewhat startled, but I tried not to show it. There

were times when Jonathon Keene seemed able to reach inside my head and read the thoughts that lay there un-
spoken. That very afternoon I had been thinking I might be
able to win a great deal of money by running this ugly
horse, but I had said nothing to Jon on the subject of racing.

"When you do," Jon said, "there are some things you
should remember. One is that many men here in the South,
particularly in Texas, breed their horses to be sprinters.
That is the kind of speed needed by a man working cattle in
heavily brushed country. They put the rider quickly into
position to throw his rope. And these men race their horses
in sprints as well. They run a course of half a mile or often
less, often only a quarter of a mile. If you match this horse
against them you will surely lose. Never run him at less than
a mile, and two miles would be even surer."

Jon grinned. "Another thing is that whenever you make a
match, each and every time, there can be but one winner.
That will not always be you.

"Never bet more than you can afford to lose, Duncan.
And when you do lose, pay your wager with good grace. A
gentleman pays his debts gracefully. See that you always
do.

"When you win, and I believe you can win often with this
horse, have the grace also to remember that the victory be-
longs to the horse, not to you. Never lord it over the loser.
The horse might have that right, but you do not."

He coughed into his hand. "Finally, you might want to
remember too that I am not the only good judge of
horseflesh there is. This particular animal was available at a
profit to you. There was a reason for that. I know Charlie
well enough to know that he judges a horse not on looks or
color, but from the hide inward."

"I can't fault this yellow," I told him quickly.

"Which only means you don't know why he was traded,
not that a reason does not exist. Remember that too."

I did, too, for Jon was a sensible man and seemed a judge

of both horses and people. I tried for days to be objectively critical of the yellow. I already knew he had speed, but now I pushed him and determined that he had stamina as well. I rode him hard through rocks and into and out of the steep-walled arroyos and washes that we had to cross. When none were in our path I went looking for rough country to attempt, and not once did I find anything the yellow would shy from or which he could not negotiate rapidly and well. He was as agile as he was fast.

Nor was he nervous about what was being done from his saddle. Jon suggested he might be impossible to work from, so I borrowed a length of rope from the wagon and swung it around my head in an imitation—although I had not the faintest idea of how to throw a loop myself—of vaqueros and cowhands I had seen at their work. So long as I was performing my feats at a standstill the horse slumbered while I played.

I tried carrying things on or around the saddle, heavy things and flapping cloth and dangling lines. He seemed not to notice them.

Finally I tried shooting my revolvers from his back, first the little .32 and then the big .44, which made a fearsome noise even if it did have a mild and not unpleasant recoil in the hand. The first shots caused the horse to twitch his ears and once go so far as to raise his head. Thereafter he ignored my noisy antics.

"Whatever it is, Duncan, I can't find it either," Jon admitted after several days of this sort of thing. That made me feel considerably better.

We continued to move and to attend to business while this was going on, and now many of the inhabitants we met were Mexicans. Jon said they and their people had been on their land since before we owned it, but their prosperity here was admittedly a hard thing for a Texas boy to accept.

Also we earned very little, they being inclined to hire no labor and to buy little. The few coins they did part with were mostly the big dollars minted in Mexico. Jon would accept their silver but not their smaller coins, although he freely gave them change in American money.

We found some white people as well, and helped to dig a well here or repair a bellows there. Whatever the task, Jon was its equal and I learned much from him about the sufficiency of one's self.

Between times I enjoyed the yellow horse and practiced with the .44, drawing rapidly now and firing for accuracy, where before I had drawn and snapped the gun without firing. In the evenings I read until the light was gone and our fire low, and often talked with Jon afterward about whatever ideas I had found in the book. It was a pleasant time.

We crossed into Arizona Territory and found more white people in the process of establishing ranches in this sparsely populated country. Here Jon's supply of salable items began quickly to dwindle and he said he would soon have to turn south toward the freight road, where the goods from the big wagons would allow him to restock.

Jon's services as a well finder were less in demand here, for the few ranchers were able to locate on available water, but his portable smithy was much in use. Most of the ranchers here were competent men who had moved in from other, more crowded places, but some were so ignorant they could not properly shoe their own horses. The mules in the trade string, hardier and more adaptable than horses, were easily exchanged for heavy draft animals that had come out of the East drawing the movers' wagons.

At one place a man who obviously was a farmer trying to become a rancher bought a few tiny items from Jon and was interrupted in his dealings by a sack-shirted child who ran to inform him that the milk cow was out of her pen again.

When I saw the poor state of the pen I began to wonder whether the man had even been a farmer, for he had expected to contain the family milch cow behind a skimpy palisade of twisted cedar poles set a foot from one to the other and not even tied together at the top. The cow, of course, had simply pushed her way through them when she decided she was hungry enough to bother.

As I had the yellow horse saddled and close to hand—and as there was a reasonably attractive daughter among the family—I immediately offered to return the cow to her confinement. Jon, in the meantime, offered to help the would-be rancher repair his corral, which meant it would be properly tied together when they were done.

I mounted the yellow with something of a flourish and wheeled him in pursuit of the brown-and-white milk cow. The gelding leaped forward at the touch of my heels and charged in the direction I gave him.

It was my intention to race past the quietly standing cow so as to startle her into motion and then to direct her homeward with the movements of the yellow, as I had seen ranchers do when bringing their animals into pens. I was in for a surprise.

The yellow dashed toward the cow, seemed to notice the beast for the first time, and thirty yards short of my target bogged his head and came to a sliding, shuddering, entirely too rapid halt.

I, unsuspecting, remained in motion.

I slid ingloriously and quite painfully down the yellow's neck and onto the ground. It was only because I was too startled to release my hold that I retained my grip on the reins.

As soon as I regained my lost breath I scrambled to my feet. The yellow horse, always so calmly imperturbable, was wall-eyed and trembling. Fear-sweat was beginning to darken its coat and to run down its forelegs from the vee of its chest. The animal was breathing more heavily than if I had just run it for four miles.

Jon came running to me and took my arm. "Are you all right, Duncan?"

I still did not have enough surplus breath to allow speech, but I did nod my head.

"You're sure? Just winded?"

I gulped in more air and said, "Sure."

Jon looked at me closely, seemed satisfied that I really was all right, and looked at my yellow horse. He began to laugh.

"It ain't funny," I protested, reverting for the moment to the old habits of loose speech he had tried to teach out of me.

"I'm not laughing about your fall, Duncan. I promise you I'm not. I'm laughing at old Charlie."

"Charlie?"

He grinned. "Now we know what faulted this horse. The fool thing is afraid of cows."

I stated some strong oaths and led the animal back toward our trade string. For the rest of the day I was quite through with riding him.

Behind me the rancher's children ran on foot to clap their hands and drive the milch cow back into her pen.

I was quite relieved when we finished with the corral repairs and were able to leave that place.

# CHAPTER 8

We moved south and hit the stage road again at a town named Casement, a place of no great size, containing perhaps fifty or sixty souls and with no obvious reason for its existence.

I expected Jon to bargain with the freighters who passed through on the highway, but he went instead to a local shop for his needs.

You kept the goodwill of local merchants better, he explained to me, if you did your buying with them instead of from their own suppliers. And he always did expect a discount price due to volume and professional courtesy. It took him very little time to make his purchases.

Outside again, while we were placing the new items into their proper storage compartments or boxes in the wagon, a freighter recognized Jon and approached us.

"Keene, isn't it?"

"Yes. And I'm sorry, but I don't remember your name, although your face is familiar."

The man stuck a hand out. "Gus Lacey, Mr. Keene. We met up in Arkansas a couple years ago."

Jon blinked twice, thought for a moment and nodded. "Of course, Gus. You bought a little dun mare from me. I hope she worked out for you."

Lacey grinned and bobbed his head. "Just what you said she was. My oldest is riding her to school and we got a good little painted filly from her that'll carry the next oldest."

"I'm glad to hear that, Gus."

"She's a decent one all right." He edged a bit closer. "You're still in the trading business, aren't you?"

"I am."

"Well looka here then, Keene, maybe you can help me out of a spot. I mean, I already know I can take your word. An' you know me too, if you see what I mean."

"Go ahead."

"The thing is, Keene, I'm hauling on my own now. I own my rigs outright and everything in them."

Jon nodded appreciatively.

"The thing is, I make out just fine every time I get a load through. But I'd be hurt bad if I lost it all."

Again Jon nodded.

"An' I been having some troubles this trip. Some Indians —they weren't but kids and they weren't carrying guns or anything, just out raising hell and looking to see what they might steal, I figure—they got into my horses one night. Got away with five head of my twelve, and I can tell you it was a blow to me. I limped in here short, but I can't make it on to California that way. I replaced two of them here but that run me out of ready cash until I get to the turnaround and sell this stuff. I'd try to peddle some of my freight along the way to make do, but it's all already consigned, and I don't want to tell a man something and then not deliver. That ain't right."

Lacey had been talking fast. He paused just long enough to draw in a deep breath and added, "Mr. Keene, would you consider selling me three head on a letter of credit? I can write you one on the Bank of Fort Smith. They know me there. They'll make it good."

The man seemed quite nervous. I was too inexperienced at the time to realize, until it was explained to me afterward, that he had admitted to Jon that he did not yet have funds in the bank to cover his draft. He would have to make up the amount when he got home from wherever he was going.

Jon did not hesitate, though. "Of course I'll take your draft, Gus. Pick out what you want and we'll talk about price."

The man grabbed Jon by both shoulders and shook him quite soundly. "God bless you, Keene. It's a marvel that we found you here." His excitement and relief were plain. He turned and called out the good news to the driver of his second wagon and to the two boys my own age or younger who were his helpers.

They and several other freighters who apparently were traveling together—I would suppose for safety, as there were said to be Indian depredations along the road from time to time—drifted over to participate in the selection of Lacey's new animals.

Not that there was a great deal to choose from. At the time our trade string held only four heavy horses, one light mule, a cow pony and, of course, my yellow horse at the end of the line where I could detach him easily for my frequent side excursions.

Any three of the four heavy horses would have done an adequate job for Lacey, but naturally there was a great deal of communal examination and speculation to be gone through before it was determined which three should be taken.

Jon and Lacey were at the center of the gathering, with the others mingling loosely nearby. I stood by the horses, awaiting requests to show off one or another of them.

While standing there I happened to overhear one of the freighters, a lean, brown-skinned man with a slouch hat and high, lace-up boots, comment on "that ugly sonuvabitch at the end of the string."

In spite of the yellow's performance with the milch cow I had become quite fond of him and could not now stop myself from retorting to the man, "If you call that horse ugly, mister, then you're no judge of horses. He might not be pretty, but he's the fastest and the best animal in this or any other territory." Which was laying it on perhaps a trifle thick, as the yellow had yet to be tested against another, but the remark had put my blood up.

"Fast?" the man returned. "Why, he's a damned scarecrow, boy. An' I'll bet his owner isn't so anxious to make claims about him." He laughed heartily and to some companions, but fully in my hearing, said, "The kid's made a pet of the poor thing, boys. It's prob'ly been in the string forever 'cause no one else would want it."

Those who had been listening got a laugh out of that. Except for myself.

"The horse is mine, by God, and I'm willing to put my money on him against any horse you care to match against him."

The vulgar person who had judged my yellow so poorly waved a hand in dismissal. "I don't wanta take your money, boy. Just forget it."

One of the listeners, apparently thinking to be helpful, touched my shoulder and said, "That's good advice, son. Forget it. That gentleman is Harry Tew and he travels with a roan that probably earns him more money than honest work ever did."

"You can keep your damn hands *and* your advice to yourself, mister." I was feeling quite hot by then. "My horse will leave his or any other, and if Harry Tew won't back his roan in a match then I say he is a lying sonuvabitch himself."

"Calm down, Duncan," Jon said at my ear, but loud enough for Tew to hear too. I hadn't noticed Jon come over, but then I guess we had been creating something of a disturbance. Tew was starting to color up and look mean, and I was plenty ready for whatever he might want to start.

"Before this gets out of hand," Jon said, "let's remember

that this started as a question between horses, not people. Tew, do you want to match your horse against this boy's?"

"It oughta be beneath him to run a scarecrow like that, but I'll do it on one condition. When the race is over I get an apology from this little smart-mouth here."

Jon showed a hint of a smile and said, "Why don't we say that when the race is over the loser apologizes to the winner for underestimating his horse."

"Same thing," Tew snapped.

"You agree to it then?"

"I do."

"Duncan?"

"You bet."

"And the stake?" Jon asked. The people nearby were crowding closer now and starting to get excited.

Tew curled his lip some and said, "Fifty dollars." It was easy enough to see that he figured a boy my age would not have anything like that kind of money. He was intending to shame me.

Well, I did have that and something more, so I said, "Done. Fifty Yankee dollars, and the loser eats crow, mister." I reached into my pocket for my purse and produced five bright yellow eagles.

"Would you hold the stakes, Gus?" Jon suggested.

I plunked my money into Lacey's hand and glared at Tew. He returned the look while he pulled out his own share of the wager and handed it to Lacey.

"We also need a course to run, boys," Jon said. "I suggest a fair test of the animals. Two miles from a standing start. Start and finish from the same point so we all can see the results."

"There's a marker about a mile east of town," someone suggested. "A cairn of rocks and a turnoff to the south."

"You could start here, ride around the marker and return," Jon said.

Tew snorted. "Damned easy way to make fifty dollars." He pointed a finger into my face. "An' don't you go forgetting the rest of the wager."

Me, I kept hold of myself and turned to get my saddle from the wagon.

# CHAPTER 9

The roan was no taller than my yellow, but much heavier-muscled and a very handsome animal. Even under a layer of road dust you could see the shine of fitness on his coat. Next to him my yellow looked, well, scarecrowish.

The roan wasn't being ridden by Harry Tew either, but by a lightweight boy of fifteen or so who was the swamper on Tew's wagon. The horse was saddled with a little postage-stamp-looking thing of the Eastern style, kind of like a sidesaddle without the knee hooks.

I was not giving away a great deal in the weight department, though. My government issue McClellan saddle would have weighed little more than their racing saddle, and I was little if any larger than Tew's jockey.

In order to warm up both horses we rode out to the rock cairn along with one of the spectators, who had volunteered to remain there so he could attest that both horses fairly rounded the marker. There would be no cheating in that regard, for if one of us failed to pass the marker the man would wave his hat, and no bets would then be paid until he returned and made his report.

Tew's horse seemed only to be used for running, for as soon as he was saddled he became anxious and somewhat unruly. My yellow, as usual, gave every appearance of being asleep whenever he was not in motion.

In the meantime there were some enterprising souls among the crowd who were making wagers. I heard some of them offering odds as much as three and four to one against my yellow. Their losses would serve them right, I decided.

The jockey on the roan horse beside me was nearly as surly as was his employer. He looked with undisguised contempt at my lean and placid yellow, slapped his own fidgeting mount with the rein ends—which only served to more unnerve the roan—and spat a stream of dark tobacco juice near enough to my stirrup to be insulting. He was still several years my junior, and I did not in any way appreciate his contempt.

"Watch yourself, boy, or I'll beat hell out of you after I'm done showing up that snide you're riding."

He did not see fit to answer, but gave me a snotty look and turned his face away. Which was just fine by me. He would be wearing a different look when we were done.

The crowd shoved nearer, Harry Tew in the fore of them, and we lined up side by side with Gus Lacey as the starter standing at the roan's head.

"Quiet, boys. Quiet down!" Lacey shouted. The sound of his voice caused the roan to leap forward and he had gone some thirty or forty yards before the jockey could regain control of him. The boy looked to be boiling with anger by the time he had the animal returned to the start and again in position.

In a lower voice Lacey announced, "You will begin at the count of three, gentlemen. Three false starts will disqualify the offending horse and forfeit the match. Agreed?"

I waited for Tew to nod before I did so myself. We were set, and I must admit that my stomach felt curiously empty even though I had eaten not many hours before.

"On the count of three then, gentlemen," Lacey repeated. "One . . . two . . . *three!*"

The roan's haunches bunched and drove even before I reacted enough to ram my heels into the yellow. Clods of hard dirt rained into my face and over the unsuspecting yellow, causing him to flatten his ears.

The yellow stretched out his neck and began to run, but he was no sprinter and the handsome roan had a lead of nearly a dozen lengths before the yellow had begun to settle to his task.

Then, though . . . ah, but it was lovely. With each reaching stride the lean yellow horse seemed able to seek more ground. His stride was low and smooth, and he gathered speed bit by bit, so easily that the gathering pace could not have been noticeable to anyone who was not on him to feel the wind in his face and to hear the roar of it past his ears. Or if there had not been another fast-running horse there against which to judge that speed.

The roan was fast, it was true, and his rapid start had given him a long lead that must have looked laughably comfortable to the spectators behind us.

I, though, could feel the easy, flowing power in the yellow I rode, and I laughed as I came nearer the hard-driving roan.

I drew up to his flank and laughed out loud so Tew's jockey could hear me and know that I was with him. On an impulse I checked the speed of the yellow and held him there, rating the roan's pace.

Before we had completed even the first mile the boy on Tew's roan went to his stick, slashing at the horse's flanks in an effort to leave me and my yellow behind. He wrung all the speed he could from the roan, but still I held my position at his flank and laughed out loud again and again to taunt him. The boy rode hunched over in desperation with his whip arm flailing while I sat upright and drew genuine pleasure from the ride.

We thundered down on the rock cairn, and I grinned and waved to the man who was judging the turn. He waved back at me.

Both horses slowed for the turn and we swept by close to the marker, both of us passing fairly on the outside of it.

Once again the roan's ability as a sprinter gave him the advantage as we regained speed, but the lead he opened this time was not nearly so great as he had gotten at the start.

Now I gave the yellow his head and booted him sharply in the ribs. Ahead of me the tired roan was already beginning to paddle a little with each reach of his forefeet. From behind I could easily see the difference in his foot action, and I knew he was done.

The yellow was not. With only the smallest amount of urging he stretched the flare of his nostrils into the wind and floated with ever greater speed over the hard road surface.

We easily reached the roan's flanks before another quarter was done and glided past him as a harness racer might pass a dray wagon. I touched the tip of my nose with a thumb as we went by and laughed at the look I received in return.

At the finish my fine yellow's lead was so great you might not have known there was a second horse in the race.

I brought the yellow around and very nearly had time to return again to the start-finish line before the roan crossed it.

There were a scant few cheers among the crowd and a great amount of disappointment. Tew looked thunderously angry.

"He shorted the marker, by God," Tew shouted.

Lacey peered down the course toward the turnback judge, then shook his head firmly. "There's no signal," he said. "It was a fair match."

"Tell them, Leon," Tew demanded. "Tell them he short-cut you."

The jockey, to give the devil his due, would not respond. He turned his head away and dismounted in silent disgrace.

"I'll have my winnings now, Mr. Tew," I said.

Gus Lacey handed back my five ten-dollar pieces and a fold of bills that had been Tew's share of the wager. I shoved them deep into my pocket.

"And now I'll have the rest of it, Mr. Tew. You'll eat some crow, sir. As agreed."

He gave me an ugly look and said, "I'll see you in hell before I bow and scrape to the likes of a smartalecky little sonuvabitch like you."

"Then I'll see you there first, by God. You've insulted my mother, and that you *will* take back."

He spoke an exceedingly vulgar word and turned his back on me.

The offense to myself and to my horse I might have borne, but never that to my mother. I said nothing more, but tossed the yellow's reins to Lacey and strode toward the wagon where my saddlebags lay.

# CHAPTER 10

I had done nothing but behave honorably toward Harry Tew and now he thought to insult me—and this after I backed with proof every claim I made. He was a low scoundrel, it was obvious, and thought he could ride roughshod over the feelings of a small and unarmed youth. Well the sonuvabitch was going to have to think again.

I yanked my saddlebags from the wagon and carried them back to the yellow, ignoring the deep, watchful silence of the race crowd.

When they saw me tying the bags in place behind my saddle they began to speak and to laugh again—some of them, I thought, a bit nervously. I glanced around at Harry Tew and caught him openly sneering at my back. That was quite all right too. I finished securing the saddle pockets and unbuckled the near pocket.

The heft and balance of the big .44 felt good in my hand. I knew it was loaded and capped, ready to fire, but nevertheless checked to ensure that this was so. I shoved the gracefully curved barrel into my waistband and turned to face Mr. Tew.

The crowd fell silent again, and I believe that Tew's eyes widened briefly before he gained control of himself.

"Duncan . . . ," Jon began.

"No!" I told him with much force. "Mr. Tew owes me. I will collect." I did not once look toward Jonathon Keene. My eyes now were only on Tew. To him I said, "You will eat crow, sir. And you will do your best to recall your insults. Go to your knees, sir, if you expect to be forgiven."

He looked quite taken aback by that idea. He turned and stared at those around him, but in fact there were fewer of them than there had been but moments before. Men were beginning silently to ease away from the presence of Harry Tew.

Tew seemed foolishly to decide that he faced only a child engaged in a childish game of bluff. He smirked and muttered an oath. He took a step forward and planted his hands on his hips.

"You're making an ass of yourself, boy. Go home and grow up. Then come see me again sometime. I don't have the time for you now."

"Then I'll kill you where you stand, Mr. Tew."

"Bull," he said. "For one thing, boy, I'm not even armed. And any more of this an' I'll call the law. Now go on home before I do it."

"I already know the John Laws, Mr. Tew. They're a bunch of murderers, sir. And liars. Like you, Mr. Tew. And you will not call me 'boy' again. You will address me properly when you make your apology."

"What you need, boy, is not an apology but a razor strop across your backside."

"Don't call me that," I warned him again. "My name is—" I hesitated, and there was of a sudden a fierce pride in me that would not allow the use of a false name. I felt good now, confident and in control. My chest and neck felt as if they were swelling larger. I felt tall and powerful, and I knew I would be very fast this day.

"My name is Jason Evers, Mr. Tew. Of Brazos County, Texas. And I will kill you where you stand if you do not deliver to me that which is mine."

"I told you already, boy. I'm not armed."

I shook my head. "I cannot accept that, Mr. Tew. You have lied to me already when you made your wager. I believe you are armed. These good men here will testify to the truth of what I say. They have heard your lies and your insults. Drop to your knees now, sir, or die."

"Boy, you're crazy as hell," he said, but so calm was I that even that did not anger me now or break my concentration.

Harry Tew shook his head. He seemed not to be able to accept that he was going to die. He lifted his hands from his hips.

It was only natural that I should assume he was reaching for a pistol. I had to assume that or risk his bullet. I turned loose of the spring-tight tension within me.

The beautiful .44 came swiftly to my hand, and it was cocked and ready before the muzzle cleared my waistband. I pointed and squeezed just as smoothly, the way I had learned to do it, and I drove a round ball of soft lead into Harry Tew's chest.

He fell writhing to the ground, but as he still moved I knew I could not trust him not to pull his pistol, and so I shot him again and this time he flopped once and lay still.

The crowd around me was very quiet. I turned to them and said, "You saw and heard it all. I shot him in defense of my own life. I did not shoot until he moved. I only did what was right."

"He wasn't armed," someone said. The voice came from behind me, from someone too cowardly to say it to my face.

"He was armed," I said, "and when he moved I shot him."

Jon stepped near and touched my elbow. "Put it away now."

I still held the .44 in my hand. I shoved it back into my waistband. "He was armed," I said.

Jon shook his head slowly and, I thought, a bit sadly. "I'm sorry. You were wrong . . . Jason." Jon turned his back and walked away.

"You're like all the rest," I shouted to the crowd. "You would lie about me too. Well by God, you wouldn't do it to my face. None of you. The devil can take you, one and all."

I took my reins from Gus Lacey's hand, and he did not look at me as I did so but turned his face aside. I knew that he, too, would lie when I was gone.

I mounted the yellow and showed my back to those brave fellows behind me. I knew none of them would have the simple courage to try to stop me. I set the yellow into an easy lope toward the east and New Mexico, back along the racing course I had so recently run in victory. I did not need those people behind me. Not any one of them.

# CHAPTER 11

I must admit to a great sense of loneliness when I left the town of Casement behind me, and it did not lessen to any appreciable extent as the miles and then the days lengthened behind me. I had been in Jonathon Keene's company for a period of several months and now found that I had enjoyed his companionship more than I had then been aware. Still, I had my own life to be about and had I fully agreed to his way I would have been required to swallow all manner of insult and degradation. At least I have always had the satisfaction of knowing that I have ever acted honorably, in all circumstances.

I passed out of Arizona Territory and back into New Mexico, where I would not have to fear the pursuit of those who might slander me. I had a good horse, a recently replenished supply of ammunition and a fair sum of money. With those I felt quite competent to face whatever might come my way.

As soon as I was able to purchase food I moved away from the main highway and wandered the lesser roads, as I had learned now to do. In due course I arrived at a military encampment and civilian outpost called Fort Sumner, garrisoned by Negro cavalry of the same low stripe as had made life unbearable for so many in Texas.

These low beings sought to make sport of a lone white youth traveling on an unbeautiful horse. I had, quite fortunately, however, arrived soon after one of their irregular paydays and with the assistance of the speedy yellow was able to more than double my wherewithal before I turned the horse northward toward the territorial capital. I am happy to be able to state as well that I was able to accomplish this without the necessity to resort to firearms for the collection of wagers placed. No doubt this was due to their recognizing my innate superiority over them, as there were no white officers and few townsmen present at the contest. It is a well-known fact, of course, that the so-called Buffalo Soldiers were decidedly inferior troops, lacking both in skill and courage, and it was well for them that they did not contest the possession of that which was rightfully mine.

I mention this uneventful sidenote only to explain how it was that I appeared in Santa Fe on the good yellow horse with nearly three hundred dollars in my pockets, yet still with little true worldly experience to bolster my growing knowledge and abilities.

The territorial capital as I found it then was a confusing warren of twisting alleys and mud-walled buildings, quite unlike the gracious and well-planned city of Austin where I had spent so many happy years in my youth.

It was my intention to take a room at the finest hostelry available to the public, but upon inquiry I was told that La Fonda was booked full in advance for some time to come. They did not give the appearance of being so busy, but I did not then know to offer payment in advance. Still, my education if not my reputation would undoubtedly have suffered had I thought to do so.

I was directed to an inn several squares distant and there indeed was able to secure a room. This establishment catered to transient workingmen such as teamsters and bullwhackers; it had a large quantity of very small and seldom-cleaned rooms available.

Being in good spirits and feeling—in my inexperience—immeasurably wealthy, I quartered my horse, left my few possessions with the innkeeper and resolved to treat myself to a new and a fine suit of clothing.

I returned to the inn that evening some forty dollars

poorer, but grandly decked out in a handsome brown suit coat with matching brown broadcloth trousers—the shelf creases carefully pressed out by a thoughtful shop owner—a black brocade vest, a boiled shirt with a string tie and a pocketful of extra collars, soft leather boots and a fine, new, low-crowned hat. I felt and undoubtedly looked the most dapper young swell in Santa Fe. It was a new sensation to me and one which I greatly enjoyed, having always before been dressed in whatever cheap garments I could come by.

I felt altogether too fine to hide myself in my room and so stopped at the inn's saloon to order my supper. As I was finishing the meal I was approached by a man who had been seated at a nearby table.

"Am I interrupting your meal?" he inquired politely.

"You are not, sir. I am quite done, thank you."

"Fine." He pulled out the chair opposite me, but offered his hand before sitting. "I am Peter B. Clawson."

"Jason Evers," I told him.

"I was just remarking to my friends, Mr. Evers, not more than an hour ago that was, how rare it is for one to see a gentleman in Santa Fe these days." He smiled. "In point of fact, Mr. Evers, a wager was made. Your appearance in this place tonight caused me to win it. Would it be too forward of me to invite you to share my good fortune?"

I had been, as already mentioned, somewhat lonely since leaving Jonathon Keene's wagon and was frankly in such good spirits that I might have welcomed conviviality from this man or from the devil himself. "I would be delighted, Mr. Clawson," I told him. I left payment for my supper and a generous tip as well and accompanied Mr. Clawson to his table. There he introduced me to two men named Ransom and Hans, and I joined their party.

My three companions were older men than I, perhaps in their thirties or forties. All three were dressed as city fellows, and I took them to be shopkeepers or civil servants or such similar types as will gravitate to a capital or a center of trade.

"You must join us for a drink, Jason. Would you care for a beer?"

I shook my head. "Not a beer, please." I had tried the stuff several times in my youth and found the flavor bitterly unpleasant.

"Whiskey then," Clawson said. "A bottle for the table, Julio, and four glasses if you please."

The Mexican waiter brought a bottle of reddish liquor and four very small, thick-sided, heavy little glasses. Clawson poured for us all.

The other three gentlemen tossed their drinks off deftly, and I did my best to imitate them. I had sipped hard liquor once before and found it to be fiery stuff, but taken this way, largely avoiding the tongue, it went warm into my stomach and left in my mouth a most enjoyable lingering aftertaste.

"Another round, gentlemen," Clawson said.

We drank like that for some little time and my new friends seemed quite pleased with my company, for they pressed upon me their goodwill and deliciously funny remarks and much smooth whiskey. We must have drunk a considerable amount, for by the time someone suggested we go visit Tia Esmeralda it was my turn to pay, and the amount was not small.

Tia Esmeralda's establishment too was a place of comfort and goodwill, with the drinks flowing freely and a number of charmingly plump Mexican ladies present to add to the jolly mood of our party.

One of these ladies, whose name I do not remember, suggested that she and I continue the party in private, and this I agreed to.

I remember—if vaguely—that there was some amount of argument about this from my friends, who expressed concern for my welfare if they were not to be with me. I remember certain solicitous comments about my youth and about the security of my purse if I were to be away from their protection.

In the end they agreed that I should go with this lady if they should be permitted to hold my purse in security for me while I was apart from them.

I was more than anxious to agree to this. There had been a certain amount of pleasurable stimulation taking place beneath the tabletop, and I do not doubt that I would then have agreed to leave with them my wits and my soul if only I should have been permitted privacy with the plump Mexican girl. In fact, of course, I had retained no wits which I could have pawned into their custody.

In the end I emptied my pockets into Mr. Clawson's open hands and accompanied the woman to a small chamber where, in the course of the party, I became acquainted with certain things that until then had been mysteries to me.

That much I remember quite well. The next memory I have is of concern that my new clothes were becoming soiled. I found myself lying full length along the foot of an adobe wall in the stifling, foul-smelling heat of one of Santa Fe's alleys. My head felt quite shattered and my stomach quite as foul within as the alleyway smelt without. It was not a joyous wakening.

# CHAPTER 12

Tia Esmeralda opened the door readily when confronted with the muzzle of my .44. She did not seem terribly much intimidated, though. She gave me a small, knowing smile as she stepped aside for me to enter.

"I want my money."

"You came to the wrong place," she said calmly.

"I don't think so. I woke up broke."

She nodded. "Hung over, too, if I'm any judge."

"It happened here. I had a lot of money on me when I walked in that door last night."

"Pah!" she snorted. "I have a fine reputation here, young man. You left with everything that was yours. Including that pistol you keep waving at me and the little one in your coat pocket. My girls let me know when you gave your money to your friends and they left while you were upstairs. I made sure we dressed you and sent you out with everything that was yours, down to and including your collar button."

I looked at the gun in my hand and fingered my collar—limp now and no doubt something less than natty—and admitted to myself that she was speaking sensibly. Had she wanted to she could have stripped me the night before and left me with nothing. I put the revolver away.

"Where can I find them?"

She shrugged. "Who knows? It is not my affair what others do or where they go afterward. You will leave now, please. Would you like a drink to help you along?"

"God, no." The thought of whiskey now was almost more

than my stomach could bear. The fact of it would have been impossible. I had not known any one human being could feel so utterly miserable and yet remain alive. I turned and walked somewhat unsteadily from her house.

I was quite disoriented and had some difficulty finding my way back to the inn, but at length managed to do so.

"Never saw them before," the innkeeper told me when I related my tale and asked about my recent companions. "You say you were picked clean?"

"I was."

"You only paid for one night. Take your things an' get out."

"I didn't even sleep in that room."

"Your business, mister, not mine. Take your things and go. Unless you have the price of another night."

I shook my head and handed him the iron key I had never really used. My saddlebags and bundle of old clothing were in a closet behind the desk, along with other bags and bundles belonging to the other guests.

"I certainly won't stay here again," I told him.

"I may never get over the loss," he said with a sneer.

I shouldered my meager burdens and left.

Fortunately I had paid in advance for the yellow's lodging also, or I would have had difficulty reclaiming him. That loss I absolutely could not have borne. I saddled and mounted him and began to wander aimlessly through the winding streets and alleys of the city.

At least I was not hungry. My stomach would have rebelled at the introduction of food, which was just as well under the circumstances as I had no money with which to buy a meal.

The longer I rode among the strangers in this ugly city the angrier I became, and the more I wanted to find those three infamous thieves so I could express my displeasure to them. Had I at that time seen any or all of them I would have opened fire on them without warning, regardless of the consequences to my life or to my reputation.

Throughout the afternoon I rode glowering through the streets, returning again and again to the square in front of La Fonda and the seedy-looking Governor's Palace as the hub of my search until finally people began to notice my recurring presence and a constable approached me.

"What are you up to here?" he challenged.

"I don't know as it's any of your damned business," I said. I could hardly state my name and concerns to him, as I had no way of knowing whether there might be flyers out on me or under what name if there were. I knew by now that my best course with the law was to keep my mouth shut and to take no water from any of the scum.

"I think that bank over there makes it my business when anybody's acting strange hereabouts. And I'd say that you are acting strange, boy."

The truth is that I had been looking at people on the streets and paying no attention to the ugly buildings of his town. I had not even realized that there *was* a bank on the square.

"There's nothing of mine in there," I told him.

"An' nothing that's in there is gonna be yours either. Now pack yourself off from here and stay gone. I intend to be watching, boy, and if you come back I'll run you in for loitering."

You'd have a hell of a time trying it, I thought, but I didn't say anything. I yet had my .44 and would not be taken, but I had enough woes for the moment and chose to ride away from him rather than risk more trouble. I am not especially proud of that episode, turning my tail to a dim-witted town constable, but I promised to be totally truthful about all matters herein. And so I turned my back and rode meekly away from that bumpkin.

Already the day was becoming late and I had no funds with which to provide for myself or my horse, and there was no open grass in the city for his sustenance. I therefore turned his head northward on the most obvious road, which happened to be the old Santa Fe Trail.

That night I dined on springwater and black thoughts while the good yellow made do with the sparse, dry grasses available there.

In the morning I shot a half-grown kid that wandered near, and I roasted a goodly portion of him to ease my hunger.

A Mexican goatherd made as if to protest, but I explained to him that the kid was already dead and should not now be wasted. I was able to impress upon him the reasonableness of my argument and my need, and as he was unarmed he gathered up his remaining livestock and herded them elsewhere.

I followed the ancient trail into the mountains—the first such grandly true mountains I had ever seen, and a curious kind of joy to my eyes—and down again long the rocky road to the famed Arkansas River, about which I had heard so much.

The river at this late season was scarcely a stream where I crossed it. I followed the well-rutted road in search of a settlement where I might hope to secure provisions or even a source of income.

The place I eventually came to was the loose grouping of traders and craftsmen who had gathered at the ruins of old Bent's Fort, which must once have been an impressively powerful outpost but now was melting back into the soil it had been built from.

There were a few wheelwrights and smiths here to service the wagons that yet used the ancient highway, and some traders who apparently took slim pickings from the blanket Indians who happened to come so far from their reserved lands in pursuit of old habits and old freedoms. I was told, too, that not all of the red men who called here were of the blanket variety and that some were as yet unreconstructed.

Of those few I personally observed I could not tell one type from the other, but found them all to be louse-ridden and bedraggled-looking creatures.

There were various encampments of both red men and white strung along the river bottom near the old fort, with the remains of the post as the hub of the activity.

I inquired there about the prospects for a race or even for a job of work, but was rejected by men whose tones said more clearly than their words that this was a story they heard all too often. One of them, however, did give me a bowl of some unidentifiable and foul-looking stuff from a stewpot and for this pittance I was grateful. Such was my low state of existence at the time.

I might well have gone on unrewarded for my efforts had not I delayed at that man's fire, but shortly after I finished my meal I was treated to the sight of a familiar face entering through what remained of the old eastern gate. It was my former companion named Hans, one of those who had guised himself as a friend only to turn and rob me.

Without thinking I leaped to my feet and cried, "Robber!"

Hans stopped where he was. He seemed quite startled.

"I'll have back what's mine or you'll die, by God."

Hans recovered his composure. To those nearby he said, "The boy's crazy. I never saw him before."

"I'll have it now," I told him.

"Go away." He turned as if to leave.

I had given him fair warning, as any honest man who was there that day can attest. I pulled the .44, took careful aim across the distance that separated us and shot him several times through the body.

It is not true that I robbed his corpse in full view of those present. I would not do such a thing as to take anything to which I was not entitled. I did recover a portion of that which had been taken from me by removing his purse from his pocket and reclaiming some forty or so of the nearly three hundred dollars that had been stolen from me. Those who have since made false accusations against me were obviously not in possession of the facts.

"This man robbed me some days ago," I told those who were still near. "This money was mine."

The man who had fed me came closer to look. He shook his head. "Do you know him?"

"Only well enough to have been his victim."

"That man was Bob Levin, and he worked for Cyrus McComb. Those boys stick together. I wouldn't go to sleep tonight if I was you, sonny."

"They can leave me be or get more of the same as this one got," I told him. "I don't much care which."

He looked at me searchingly and asked, "Who are you, boy?"

"My name is Jason Evers, and your Mr. Cyrus McComb can step aside when he sees me coming, by God."

"I'll tell him you said so."

"You do that." I pocketed my money and walked away toward the traders so I could buy the things I needed.

# CHAPTER 13

I didn't have to wait until dark for the McComb gang to come for me. Not that I would have run from the likes of them anyway.

They approached me in the full daylight of the late afternoon, sneaking up behind me as I was engaged in tying a sack of foodstuffs behind the cantle of my saddle. So blatant were they about their intent to murder an innocent traveler that they made their approach within view of probably seventy-five to a hundred men who were engaged in business there near the old fort or who had stopped at the popular resting place for some other reason. The actual site, for those who may be curious, was approximately one hundred fifty paces toward the river from the southeast corner of the fort ruins. Had I known in advance what would transpire there I would have gone in the other direction from the ruins, to the old post cemetery.

I was facing the ruins across the narrow rump of my hard-used yellow when McComb and four of his henchmen moved up from the river bottom to my rear. The first knowledge I had of them was when McComb spoke my name. I can only thank the presence of so many strangers as having provoked this seeming courtesy, as I have no doubt that under other circumstances McComb would have shot me in the back where I stood, without warning or opportunity for defense.

"Jason Evers," the voice came. "Turn around."

I did so and for the first time faced this man.

"I am Cyrus McComb," he said, "and today you killed one of my men."

"Today I killed a thief who had robbed me. Do you claim him then?"

"Bob Levin was no robber," he said. "But you are a murderer. I heard about you in Texas, Jason Evers. You did murder there too, but I have not yet heard of you killing anyone who was capable of defending himself. Well, I am quite capable, boy. This time you have to face a man who will be shooting back at you."

Obviously the man thought to turn the onlookers his way by making such base and groundless accusations, but it would not work. For if my name was known in Texas, Cyrus McComb's was known there and through many of the southwestern territories.

McComb was a man who had appeared in north Texas some time before the defeat of the gallant South. He had appeared from somewhere to the east with gold in his pockets and no explanation of how he had come by it. There were some who said he had been a high-ranking Confederate officer who abandoned his men but kept their pay and thereby greatly harmed the glorious Cause, but no one knew for sure.

He had taken up land, using state and Republic of Texas scrip, buying from war-destitute families at a cent an acre or little more, and both his wealth and his cattle herds increased at a marvelous rate.

It was said of him that he was a livestock thief and much worse, but none of this was said to his face, for he was known to be a man of intemperate moods and fierce anger. It was well known that McComb's employees were instructed to shoot or hang anyone tampering with McComb beef, no matter who they were or how great their need. Twice he had stood much-publicized trial on charges of murder and each time had managed to wriggle free of the noose. It was said of him that he set great store by the jury system. Great store . . . and high prices.

He was a frequent thorn in the side of the legislature as well—as I knew from my residence in the capital city—and was a man who had far more than his share of enemies.

This, then, this would-be empire builder who I later learned was on his way home from delivering beef to the boom towns of Colorado Territory, was the man who had the temerity to stand and cast accusations at an innocent youth.

Possibly he thought that the wealth he carried in his saddlebags could buy him out of trouble here, too. I shall never know.

Whatever his intentions, he stood there and made his false statements, and I looked into his face and laughed out my defiance. "You said you would face me, Mr. McComb, but I see four of your hired killers with you. I suppose that is as fair a fight as the likes of you would offer."

"You shot Bob down in cold blood."

"I gave the robber full warning of what I would do if he failed to make good what he stole from me without warning not a week ago down in Santa Fe."

"Bob Levin hadn't been out of my company in the past month and a half, boy, and I haven't been down to Santa Fe in more than a year."

"Lies won't change the facts, Mr. McComb, no matter how often you repeat them. A man your age should know that." That was a thing Jonathon Keene had told me once, and I had not forgotten it.

"That's right, boy. And I told the truth," he insisted. "I intend to take you now, Evers. Or you can submit to a trial by your betters, right here and now. You have the choice. I would accept the judgment of these good men around us." He passed a pointing hand dramatically around him toward those who were watching us.

"I would trust their fairness, McComb, but I'm not fool

enough to trust you or your assassins. I will lay my gun down for no man, and especially not for a man like you who is known to be a murderer. If you intend to do murder here you cannot expect help from your victim."

"I intend to do justice here."

"All five of you to face a boy you have already accused as a coward?"

"No, by God. Myself alone. And the ghost of Bob Levin." He turned his head toward his men. "Boys, you stay out of this. I'll have no man say this wasn't fair when it's done."

The men behind him looked unhappy over this, but he fixed his glare on them one by one until he had a nod from each. With that he turned back to me. "The final judgment is coming for you, Jason Evers," he said.

"Not now, I think, but I will happily argue my case when the time comes."

Cyrus McComb's hand moved toward his holstered pistol and my own good .44 came swiftly into my hand and leaped in recoil.

My ball flew higher than I intended and struck him in the forehead instead of the breast. The impact of it snapped his head backward and flung him down so that he was no longer on his feet when I fired the second time.

That ball flew through the space where McComb had been standing and found a mark in the chest of one of his men.

The other hired thugs, thinking themselves fired upon after their leader's death, drew their own weapons.

Although there were still three of them unharmed and sound of body, I had a certain small advantage in that my .44 was already in my hand. I fired at the one to my right, missed and fired again. My ball struck him in the groin and he fell.

I fired yet again, this time at the one in the center, and had the satisfaction of seeing my shot take effect in the area of his jaw. He began bleeding profusely.

By this time the last of McComb's men was shooting at me. I was aware of his fire, but curiously remained unafraid of it. I felt somehow certain that his balls could not find me.

I aimed my pistol at this man's breast, but the gun snapped empty. I shifted it to my free hand and hurriedly drew the little rimfire .32 from my coat. All the while he continued to shoot toward me.

It has been said that I shot this man, Richard Tramwell by name, after his pistol had been emptied and he found himself without defense. I can say in all genuine honesty that in the heat of this combat I did not pause to count my own shots and far less would I have kept count of his. As soon as the little Smith was in my hand I used it to shoot him three times through the body. I agree that he did not fire more shots at me *after* that occurrence.

Several of McComb's men were lying wounded on the ground but were yet alive, so I made haste to reload my .44 and paid no immediate attention to the carnage before me. Afterward I could not with any degree of certainty know which fallen firearm had belonged to whom. I therefore must plead myself a poor witness as to whether Tramwell should still have been considered armed and dangerous at the time of his death, which I freely admit he reached at my hands and by the skill of my arms.

The final toll of that famous and much misunderstood fight, about which I now set down the true facts for the first time, was that Cyrus McComb and Richard Tramwell were killed outright in the affray which they themselves had initiated. The man who had been standing to the rear of McComb, and who accidentally fell victim to my second bullet, suffered a mortal wound and expired within a matter of hours.

Donald Clench, also written as Donald Clinch in certain accounts, recovered from his groin wounds and as far as I know retired from the public eye thereafter.

Caleb Donner, unrelated to the famous Donner Party of

human flesh-eating notoriety, recovered from his disfiguring jaw wounds to become a most vitriolic—and grossly unjust—critic of my role in the affair. It has been he who, through the time intervening, has granted countless interviews with sensation-mongering scribes and who has succeeded in distorting the true facts in the minds of those who believe they know what transpired that day.

I can ascribe this injustice only to the fact that Donner himself was maimed and heavily scarred by my ball and thus has ever after been forced to shave around a constant reminder of my success against him. This, I suspect, has left him embittered, and in understanding this I now am able to find it within my heart to forgive him his slanders and false charges.

I do, however, note that it is only Donner's word that places Bob Levin, previously known to me as Hans, in Colorado when in fact he was in New Mexico Territory and there engaged in the robbery of an innocent young man.

I would note also that upon having free access to the coin and currency of Cyrus McComb I announced my intentions to the crowd assembled and took from his packs only the three hundred dollars due me. I directed that the remainder, a sum of several thousand dollars, be transmitted to McComb's widow with my regrets.

# CHAPTER 14

I would be far less than honest if I did not admit here and now that it was this much-discussed fight which made my name one to be heard and remembered wherever men would gather and which did much to make me the public figure I have become.

It was not so much, I believe, the fight itself—although a lone man facing five armed and murder-bent gunfighters is certainly no mean feat—as it was my bold and generous gesture in returning McComb's fortune to his widow that made the incident such a popular one.

It was not harmful either that Cyrus McComb was a man much hated by his enemies and envied by his neighbors, a man often accused—accurately, I am sure—of heinous crimes and countless wrongdoings.

Whatever the rationale, though, of those who heard the story, the tale had already preceded me by the time I reached Kansas and the newly blossoming cow towns. There I was greeted as something of a celebrity, and in truth I quickly learned to enjoy this distinction.

It was well that I had been able to recover my fortune, modest though it was, for the stout yellow horse upon which I depended so heavily had suffered a grazing wound in the near flank during the McComb affray. The injury was not severely damaging, but it did, of course, prohibit me from racing the fine animal lest I cause him serious damage or—quite as bad—cause him to lose heart from an inability to outrun his competitors.

I traveled slowly therefore, and arrived in the town of

Abilene with a full purse and a healthy if still not race-fit horse.

I had learned my lesson about the patrons in the poorer hostelries and put up in a decent-looking inn called the Drover's Rest. Immediately upon registering I was greeted with recognition, and the clerk summoned the proprietor, a man named Samuel Todd, to make my acquaintance.

Todd introduced himself and said, "You registered as Jason Evers. Might I ask if you have recently come from Colorado Territory, perhaps from the Bent's Fort region?"

I admitted that indeed I had.

He shook his head and said, "I would not have guessed to find you such a young-looking man, Mr. Evers. Not after the accounts we heard here about your prowess as a gunfighter, sir. Could I ask how old you might be? If you would not find the question offensive, that is."

Now I was not greatly used to such courteous and considerate treatment, and I was more than willing that it should continue. Also I had had quite enough of being called "boy" by all and sundry strangers. I therefore gave my age as twenty and three, adding slightly more than five years to my true age, as I was then within a few days of my eighteenth birthdate. This trivial incident may well account for much of the confusion among my would-be, and often inaccurate, biographers.

"Have you had your dinner, Mr. Evers?" Todd asked.

It was already well past the noon hour, but I had been on the road and had not stopped. I told him this.

"I would be honored if you would join me as my guest," he said.

This I was quite willing to do. The hotel proprietor had a boy carry my things to a superior room while he himself led me to his own reserved table in the dining room adjacent to the small lobby.

Mr. Todd ordered for us baked oysters under a green sauce, portions of roast goose, certain other delicacies equally foreign to me and my first taste of wine. Whatever the label—and I had not then the knowledge to know or even to care—it was of a fine and delicate flavor that even now I could not fault. I quickly learned that I had a taste for the finer and more genteel pleasures that life has to offer, and for this I remain grateful to Samuel Todd.

During our meal he excused himself for his curiosity and proceeded to question, from the horse's mouth as it were, the accuracy of the reports that were being broadcast about the McComb affair.

"Is it true, Mr. Evers . . . ?"

"Jason," I told him.

He smiled. "Is it true, Jason, that you challenged seven of them in a face-to-face encounter? And there was only one survivor? One bullet per man in your six-shooter?"

"There were only five," I corrected modestly, "and I had a second pistol in my pocket. Two survived, although they were seriously wounded. And the truth is that I did not challenge them. I am not a seeker of trouble, Mr. Todd. They tried to creep up behind me in ambush, but I discovered them. Otherwise I should not be here with you today."

"The pleasure is mine, Jason, believe me."

Todd soon excused himself from the table and left me to enjoy the excellent wine at my leisure. He hurried out of the hotel, I believe to tell his cronies about his friendship with such a famous person as Jason Evers. I was, I admit, quite content with my reception in Abilene.

I was somewhat tired from my travels, so spent the rest of the afternoon in my room, which was by far the nicest I had ever seen, much less used. I napped soundly and, when I wakened, brushed my clothes to their best appearance and went downstairs.

Todd and two friends were lounging in the lobby. Todd waved me over to them and introduced his friends as Thomas Bergen and Alfred Noble. He also invited me to join their party for supper, which I was glad to do.

Once again I was asked to tell my tale. In exchange for such an excellent meal as we again had I really did not mind a few questions. As I had twice been his guest I now ordered wine for Todd and his friends, and this was popularly received by all. Our dinner took on the aspects of a celebration, and others began to join us with myself as the center of attention. We ended the evening at a place called Madame LaFleur's, and I felt myself quite fortunate to have made so many influential new friends, as my companions that evening and for some days to come were among the cream of Abilene's business society.

There were few herds of beeves in the vicinity so late in the shipping season, but I did meet a few cattlemen and a somewhat greater number of beef buyers. They too proved to be friendly, in particular the Texas cattlemen, most of whom said that their fair state was the better for being rid of Cyrus McComb and his greedy enterprises.

After not more than a few weeks of this high living, though, I realized that my purse was shrinking quite rapidly. While the three hundred dollars I had arrived with would normally be considered a year's wage, I had been accepting many social engagements and as a matter of common courtesy had felt obligated to stand treat in return. Also Madame LaFleur's place was no common bawdy house or crib row, and my bills there rose rapidly. I therefore began to keep my ear open for opportunities to derive some income. The yellow horse would have provided such opportunity, but was not yet fully recovered from his wound.

Such an opportunity arose late one evening-shank as I was leaving Madame LaFleur's and chanced to pass through the vestibule at the same time as a commission beef buyer named Ronald Sepin.

I was already acquainted with Mr. Sepin and was not greatly surprised by his greeting and suggestion that I join him for a nightcap before retiring. I accepted and walked with him to the house he had rented for the buying season now ending. There he made me comfortable in a cozy study and poured for both of us a mild Madeira.

"I've been thinking for several days about having a talk with you, Jason," he began. "I have a problem, a business problem, that you might help me solve."

"You know I would be glad to if I can," I told him freely.

"Do you know Ellis Runkel?"

"I have seen the gentleman several times. I could not say that I know him well." Runkel was a cattle drover who had recently delivered a very large herd here for rail shipment. It was expected that his would be the last shipment of consequence to move from Abilene that season.

"You may have heard, then, that I bought his beeves and paid off in cash. They were loaded on the cars and moved yesterday."

I shrugged. If I had received the information it had made little impression. Cows and the people who raised them were not of great importance to me.

"Yes, well, the thing is this way, Jason. I got a wire today saying those animals were not as they were represented to be. There may be some question of ownership, and my company might become involved in a dispute at law."

That concern I understood very well, and I told him so.

"In the meantime Runkel has already received cash payment for the beeves and if the matter goes against us—through no fault of our own, I emphasize, since we made the purchase in good faith—we would have to stand the loss. I hope you understand the seriousness of the situation."

"Of course," I assured him. "If the man misrepresented his right to sell the animals he has taken your money in exchange for something that was not his. It would be a matter of theft, actually."

"Precisely," Sepin said earnestly. "Refill?"

"Please."

He poured for us again and resumed his seat. "Normally,"

he went on, "I would go immediately to the authorities here to have the cash impounded and placed in escrow until the matter is settled at law. Then the money would be released to the proper party, my company or Mr. Runkel or the owners-in-fact of the beeves shipped."

He paused as if waiting for a response, so I nodded my head to show him I was following his discussion.

"Unfortunately, in this case the cattle have already been shipped across the state line, so there is a question of jurisdiction. That question must be resolved before any of the rest of it can be considered. And in the meantime it is Mr. Runkel's intention to depart for Texas early tomorrow morning. With my company's cash in his possession. That would complicate the jurisdictional question even further. We would have to involve the authorities in three separate states, and frankly the mess might never be straightened out if that were to happen."

"I can see that that would be a problem."

"It could be," he said, "unless someone were to convince Mr. Runkel that he should leave the cash on deposit with me until such time as its proper ownership should be established."

"Someone," I repeated.

Sepin coughed into his fist. "Perhaps someone who would not be intimidated by Mr. Runkel's reluctance to leave the money here. Or by his, uh, well-known violent nature. I was, uh, thinking that you might not be intimidated by the man, Jason."

"I don't think I would be."

He smiled. "Your assistance would be worth as much as, uh, two hundred dollars, I think."

"You said Runkel is leaving in the morning?"

"He plans to travel alone. His road crew has been paid off. It might be better to approach him when he is not surrounded by his friends. They might not . . . understand the situation."

"And you would pay two hundred dollars?"

"I might be able to manage two fifty."

"I would be glad to help you, Mr. Sepin."

We shook hands, and he poured us each a last glass of the wine.

# CHAPTER 15

I had thought to make this an easy matter on myself, getting up early and catching Runkel before he had time to ride far from his camp. Unfortunately, however, it has always been my habit to sleep as late as time might permit, and on this morning the late-night pleasurements and even later conversation betrayed me. By the time I awakened it was past dawn and I knew I had missed my man.

I therefore took a few extra minutes to assemble some belongings into my saddlebags, along with a small store of foodstuffs in case I should remain out overnight.

The yellow horse was being well maintained at a public stable, and his recent inactivity left him eager for travel. I took him out to where Runkel's camp had been and set him into a lope to the south.

The road was well marked by the beat of cattle hooves even though the trail had only recently come into use, and I had few doubts that I could find Ellis Runkel somewhere along its path.

Sure enough, in the afternoon I found the remains of a fire smoldering at what might have been his nooning place, and that evening I saw a burning campfire with a single horse staked beside it. The horse had to be a good one to have covered so much ground in a day.

I approached the fire and was pleased to find my man beside it.

"Come in," he said when he espied me. "Evers, isn't it? Sure. I saw you up in Abilene. Climb down and join me."

He introduced himself and offered coffee and proved

himself to be a friendly fellow. I began to think it a shame that I had to cramp his scheme and return the cash to Ronald Sepin.

We drank the hot, bitter coffee and I used his already dirtied pot to prepare my supper. All the while he spoke glowingly of the prospects of this new beef-trailing venture.

"It will be the salvation of Texas, Evers. The people have had no cash money for too many years and no market for all the animals that were let to run wild in the thickets. Half of them now are unowned and free for the gathering. A young man with grit and enterprise could start his fortune down my way. The hard work of the gather would be repaid in hard money." He smiled. "You're a young man yourself, Evers, and while you have a reputation, it's not one that will buy your land or shelter your woman, is it?" He winked at me. "You might give a thought to cattle hunting. I'd be willing myself to buy what you gathered for me, and I would take the risks of the trail herding, which I intend to do anyway. I'll be back up the trail next year, you see, and so will four times the number as went this season. The south of Texas is still skeptical of the thing, but I intend to tell them different. Next year this trail will be like a river of moving beeves, and with the money and the importance of our traffic to the railroads will come our way out from under the carpetbag Reconstructionists. Wait and see if I don't tell you the truth, Evers. Mark my words in your mind. The money will give us power in politics as well as in the marketplaces. So mark it well. And in the meanwhile give a thought to gathering cattle for me. You're a young man and seem a bright one. You could do well in this trade."

Now throughout all this and more I had played the role of listener, not of talker, and I was entirely too polite to speak my mind to him now.

His enthusiasm, though, failed to spark a kindred fire in my breast. I had seen ranches and more than enough ranches in my travels with Jonathon Keene and I wanted none of the dry, dusty, lonesome places for my own. I had seen their shelter, and I wanted no mud-daubed hovel or single-room shanty to call mine. Moreover, I had seen their women, as drab and lifeless as their land and their shelter, and by now I could draw comparison between those thin-lipped wives and the laughing, red-cheeked, energetic fillies I could find at Madame LaFleur's or Tia Esmeralda's or any of a hundred other such.

And I knew something, too, of what he had not said, for his comment about hard work had not so much as hinted at the truth. I had seen the ranchers and their sons and their hired men at the end of the day's work when they came in sweat-plastered and dirty, thorn-scraped and sometimes gored or kicked by their stupid bovines. They were men with twisted limbs and often-broken bodies and the smell of sweat and poverty always around them.

No sir, I answered Runkel in silence, you cannot tempt me to such a miserable life as following the backside of a cow. I had come to know gaiety and the finer things, and I would not turn now to the indignity of such stoop labor. I did not so much as have a horn on my saddle, and I wanted none. Thank you, Mr. Runkel, but no. And anyway, you will not be coming back north next season. You very soon will be a dead man.

I finished my meal and had more coffee and waited while my host cleaned up his pots—he insisted on doing the chore, and if he did not then I would have to—before I brought up the reason for my visit.

"By the way, sir," I told him, "I heard it up in Abilene that Mr. Sepin had trouble in Missouri about the ownership of those cattle you sold him."

"Huh!" he snorted. "I gave him the brand sheets and powers of attorney to cover every head. If he went and lost them he's an idiot. Which he might be. No matter, though. They're all on file with the county clerk down home. I'll write and let Sepin know where to find them. It's a good thing you told me that or I might never have heard."

It was a fine bluff and smoothly offered, and it might have taken me in had I known no more of the story than I told him. As it was, of course, I was well onto him.

"Mr. Sepin has asked that you return his money until such time as the matter is settled," I said.

He looked quite angry and opened his mouth as if to offer a retort, but he thought better of whatever he might have said. The anger on his features dissolved and twisted instead into a grin. "Hell's bells, there's no point in getting mad with you. But that Sepin sure is a stupid man to blame me for his own problems. Maybe I won't write that letter after all."

"You won't have to," I told him. "And it's all right if you want to get mad at me. I'm the one who was hired to bring the money back."

Ellis Runkel turned white, which quickly shaded to dark red. He spoke again and became abusive, the particulars of which do not bear repeating. He was not truly the friendly man he had seemed.

"Nevertheless," I said when he finally ran out of abuses and insults, "I have come to take back what is due."

"And me? What am I supposed to do?"

I shrugged. "Whatever you wish. Surrender the money to me and ride with me back to Abilene if you want. Or go home to Texas. I was hired to return Mr. Sepin's money to him. Beyond that I really don't care."

Once more he became abusive, perhaps even more so than before, as this time his invective was directed toward me more than to Sepin.

When he seemed again quite done I asked, "Will you hand it over now or must I take it?"

"You know the answer to that, you little sonuvabitch."

This sweat-smelly cowman must surely have known that

he was no match for my skill, but he was game. And I must admit he took me by surprise and came near to undoing me.

He had been squatting near me with a just-scrubbed pot in his hands and, rather than dropping the utensil to reach for his revolver—as I quite expected him to do—he instead flung the steel pot toward my unprotected face.

The pot struck the left side of my head, and only the presence of my hat prevented it from causing a nasty wound. As it was I suffered a slight gash on the left temple and was thrown off balance by his unprovoked assault. And I *had* told him he was welcome to accompany the impounded cash back to Abilene. There was no need here for gunplay.

I fell to the side, but managed to twist the .44 from my waistband as I fell. I ended sprawled on the ground with my gun in hand, as his was by then. And in truth he had been far quicker in gaining his than I expected.

Once again I saw the fire-bloom of a pistol aimed toward me and this time could feel its passage, so near the ball came to my neck. My shot was the more accurate, though, and opened up a small, red hole in his chest. The second did likewise in his belly.

Runkel dropped forward onto his knees and must have known he would be dying from his wounds. The hate on his face was a fearsome thing, and I could not trust him to die peacefully and with dignity in his final moments.

I would, of course, have eased his passing had I been allowed to do so. I had wanted none of this, and he had brought it all upon himself. Still, his gun remained in his grasp and I could not trust his attack to abate. I regained my feet and shot him carefully through the head so as to remove the danger to myself.

His body fell face forward into the fire and I hastened to roll it aside lest it come to unnatural harm. I was not then nor ever have been a vindictive or unfeeling sort of man.

# CHAPTER 16

I gave Runkel a decent burial, of course, but first went through his things. He could have no use for them, after all, and the alternative would be to let them lie, to be taken by the next passing stranger.

There were several items that could be of use to me: a nested set of steel pots in place of the more common and far heavier iron articles, a folding knife with a blade that locked open so as not to turn on bone and snap shut across the fingers, a pocket purse containing a small quantity of gold coin. These things I removed from the body prior to interment.

The man's saddlebags were the reason I had been sent in search of him, and these I inspected next.

In truth I expected a great weight of coin or a heavy bulk of paper currency. I was considerably surprised when I hefted the bags and found them nearly empty.

The one pocket held a sack of tobacco, a whetstone and a flask of spirits. The other held gloves, two pairs of unsoiled socks and a leather wallet stuffed full of papers and a small amount of currency. That was the entirety of it, for I carefully checked his bedroll and food sack also and found no sign of Ronald Sepin's cash.

I went through the papers in his wallet and found that most of them had to do with brand inspections and recordings, others with authorization for Runkel to dispose of livestock in the names of various owners and cattle companies. A few seemed to be banking statements; they indicated that Ellis Runkel had been a man of considerable wealth, his cow-smelling appearance notwithstanding. These papers I had no interest in and burned so as not to become involved in any investigation of the man's disappearance. I had, of course, done nothing improper here, but bitter experience had taught me to place no faith in either the law or its administrators. I can stand the test of any of my true actions, but no man can defend himself against false accusers. This much I knew to be true.

The only paper of interest to me and which I therefore retained was the bill of sale for the buckskin gelding he had been riding. The paper was made out not to Runkel but to a Theodore Isley and had been later signed over by him to "bearer"—which now was myself. I therefore came into possession of an undistinguished but honest pony which I thought to use as a pack animal, thus saving my good yellow for better things.

The currency and coin that had been in his possession I determined to keep as well, for between them they totaled little more than two hundred dollars. This was nearly the amount owed me by Sepin, which I was now less likely to collect due to Sepin's own misinformation about the location of his missing cash.

I put Runkel's bedroll, saddle and other unwanted articles underground near him and spent the remainder of that night beside the welcome warmth of the fire. The time of year was late enough that while no serious cold had yet set in, the nights were uncomfortably chill.

In the morning I gathered up my horses and the few things of my camp and began the ride northward toward Abilene.

Ronald Sepin was a very angry man. He cursed and ranted for some time and eventually worked himself into such a state that he began abusing me as well as my report. At that time I began to become annoyed.

"*Shut up!*" I barked in as frosty a manner as I could, and the man obeyed.

That was, I think, perhaps the first time I had ever dared to actually give orders to a grown man—after all, I was just turned eighteen despite my accomplishments and reputation—but the effect was immediate. Not only did Sepin hush himself, but he became quite white-faced when confronted with my irritation. It was a thing I knew I should remember.

"Now you just sit still and listen to me for a minute, mister," I told him. "I don't know what became of that money. I don't even know there *was* any money. I have only your word for that, and so far your word seems mighty poor.

"Now the facts are these, mister. You asked me to do a job for you. I did it. If it turned out badly for you it was because you got your information wrong, not because I failed my end of the job. So the fact is that I figure you owe me two hundred fifty dollars. And if you figure you can back out on me now, then I figure I'm just the boy to change your views, *sabe?*"

Sepin began to look quite sickly at that, and just for extra emphasis I fingered the butt of the .44 in my waistband.

The man before me put on something that I think was intended to be a smile, although it looked more like an attack of heartburn than good humor.

"Of course," he said. "I was carried away by my disappointment. I sincerely did not mean to, uh, impugn your integrity, Mr. Evers. Not at all." He looked a tiny bit brighter and said, "Now that I think of it, you mentioned he was carrying bank papers in his wallet. He might have purchased a draft, you know. He might have been carrying a bank's paper in place of cash. That could be it, Mr. Evers. You, uh, didn't think to bring . . . ?"

"I told you. I burned them."

"Are you . . . ?" He held up a hand quickly. "No. I'm sorry. Of course you are sure of what you did. Of course."

He looked thoughtful. And very worried. "What about the . . . other remains?"

"Below ground. Not marked. By spring there won't be a trace left. The herds coming north next season will walk right over him." I grinned. "He might like that, come to think of it."

Sepin looked even whiter. The fake smile slipped a bit and kind of twisted. He was plainly frightened of me. But he just couldn't leave it alone. "He might have had, you know, a money belt. Something."

"Go teach your grandmother to suck eggs, Sepin. Of course I looked for a money belt. Also the belt in his pants loops. And his boots. And the sweatband in his hat. If he'd been carrying anything I would have found it. He wasn't. I didn't. And there she lies, mister. Plain as that."

"Yes, well, it was just a thought," he said lamely.

"Sure," I said. "While you're thinking now, how about my fee?"

"He must have had some pocket money."

"What of it?" I fingered the .44 again.

"Nothing. Not a thing. That, uh, wasn't part of our agreement, was it?"

"No, it wasn't."

"Right, well, sit still there. Just relax. I'll get your fee."

"Fine."

"Don't worry about a thing." He seemed incapable of shutting himself up.

I grinned at him. "I don't worry much at all."

It was hard to believe how a man already so pale could get paler still, but he managed. If he had had any thoughts about trying to pull something on me he was forgetting them now. He walked stiff-legged and shaky across the small room and pulled out his desk chair. Just for the hell of it I got up and followed to stand over him while he fumbled in a lower desk drawer.

There was a pepperbox pistol in the drawer and probably

some kind of small stinger on his person, but he was very careful of his moves in reaching instead for a gray steel lockbox. He counted twenty-five crisp tens off of a stack of currency in the box and replaced his cache in the drawer with just as much care that I should not misunderstand and think he might be reaching for the gun. He locked the drawer when he was done, but he need not have bothered. I was not so stupid now as I had been, nor so unsuspicious of my companions. I was sure if I ever chose to come back and look I would not find the box in that same drawer again.

Sepin turned with no trace of a smile and handed me my money. "That makes us quits," he said.

"Yes, it does, Sepin, and it can stay that way. Unless, of course, you get stupid."

His eyebrows hiked up a notch.

"A few minutes ago you were saying you thought I got Runkel's money and decided to keep it."

He started to protest, but I cut him short.

"That is exactly what you were getting at, Sepin, with or without those exact words. Now I won't try to tell you I wouldn't have been tempted if things had worked out that way. The fact is that they didn't. If I was going to take all that kind of money, though, I'd do it and run. I wouldn't come back here where you might have a chance to lay for me and get your hands on it. So I brought you back an honest report and I collected an honest fee for my work. If you have any sense at all you will accept the truth of that and leave it be. And, mister, don't you *ever* link my name either to yours or to that of Ellis Runkel. If I ever hear that you have, I will come for you. Understood?"

He nodded.

And I did what turned out to be a very stupid thing, although I had no way of knowing that at the time. I walked away from that room and away from that house and I left Ronald Sepin alive behind me. The same Ronald Sepin who now is circuit court judge sitting at Manitou Springs, Colorado.

Had I had enough foresight that night I could have saved countless innocent men from jail and worse, for Sepin's reputation for dishonoring the bench is widely known. I accept no small measure of blame for this failing.

# CHAPTER 17

I had an ample stake and in the yellow horse a means to increase it. I drifted eastward for a time, into Missouri and eventually down into Arkansas. I cared little for either the country or the people who chose to live there, but I was making a fine income—spending it quite as fast as I could gain it, too—and so kept it up. I wintered that way in the areas where season-idle farmers had time on their hands and might wish to match a race to add some excitement to their lives and, so they thought, some cash to their purses.

The way I worked it out was this. Now that I had another horse I allowed the homely but marvelously fast yellow to do his traveling with only a light load of bedroll, food and my few steel pots on his back. I mounted myself on the buckskin for my daily travel.

When I found a likely place or saw a likely horse I would enter into conversation with the locals and would soon pretend to be in my cups—drunk, if you prefer—although I had well learned that lesson and would not again exchange my wits for the flavor of whiskey.

While so engaged I would in my apparent drunkenness boast that I came from country where horses were fast, that the local speedsters would have found themselves pulling a schoolmarm's gig there, that my packhorse could outrun any animal hereabouts—wherever hereabouts might have been. And sometimes I did not even know where it was I was making my brag.

At any rate, following this rude proclamation I would dig deep into my pocket and slam down fifty or a hundred dollars to back my claim. Without fail there would always be some fool who would want to take five or ten dollars of whatever I staked, and soon the entire amount would be at wager.

It then would be time to switch my old McClellan to the yellow and prove up on my boasts. From time to time the losers would be unhappy, but I never found them to be serious about it. I always offered them double or nothing on another run, but rarely had a taker. It is a fact that a man who will pull a gun when he is gulled at cards will but shake his head and pay his money when you run in a fast horse on him . . . so long as you do have the faster horse in the race, that is. And the yellow was fast enough and my farm-country scheme shrewd enough that I never once that winter faced a faster horse than mine.

As I said, I made the money freely and spent it rapidly and with pleasure. My horses and myself received the best of care. I took in Kansas City and stayed there long enough to see the sights and to have my old .44 converted from powder-and-ball to the much faster loading .44 rimfire cartridge, a conversion coming much into vogue then, as no decent guns were being made to carry cartridges. The gunsmith explained that this had something to do with patent rights. Not that I greatly cared. The .44 Army fit me just fine and now was as modern as tomorrow too. I also bought from the same man one of the new Winchester rifles, model of 1866, which fired the same fine cartridge as my refurbished revolver.

Wherever I went and wherever I found myself at night I always paid well for my bed and board, and no man could ever say that I cheated him or failed to give exactly what I owed and often beyond. Only once did I take more than I gave, and that was not of my doing. That was at a southern Missouri farmstead owned by a family named Carlston.

It was early evening when I arrived there, feeling both tired and jubilant for that morning I had run two races and won something over three hundred dollars, most of it from a single stubborn individual who had insisted that his second horse, still fresh, could outrun my once-raced yellow and offered two-to-one in proof. Not all of his neighbors had agreed with him, so I had not even left a completely unhappy crowd behind me.

I rode into the Carlston farmyard that evening and expansively offered five dollars for a soft bed, a light supper and a stout breakfast. The spade-bearded Carlston accepted with an eager light in his eye at my mention of money.

He led me into the house and, although we were already indoors, bellowed loudly, "Old woman, turn the mattress and plump the pillows for this young gentleman. You kids, you sleep in the barn tonight, your ma an' me will have the loft. Emmy, you tend the gentleman's horses. He's paying five dollars hard money and he gets our best, you hear?"

There were but two children in the house and both of them girls. One was a skinny, poorly clothed sprite of seven or so and the other just as skinny, but old enough to have her hair out of braids and into a woman's bun. Her dress was still a girl's, though, being a sacklike thing to which scant attention had been paid in its manufacture. It was this older one who bolted for the door at the call of "Emmy," barely slowing enough to hear what was being ordered before she was out and gone.

"If you don't mind, Mr. Carlston, I will go along to see to my animals. I am particular about them."

"Whatever you want, young man. Go ahead."

The yellow deserved the best and I would have been remiss had I left his care to a slip of a girl whose training I did not know. I went out onto the stoop and got there just in time to see my horses' rumps disappearing into a dark barn. If nothing else, the girl was quick to move.

Each animal was in a stall when I reached the barn, and the girl was kneeling on the floor with a striker and tinder.

"I have some matches," I offered.

"Lordy, don't waste 'em, mister. I'll have this done in no time."

"If you'd rather."

She got her spark handily and let it brighten into flame. From this she lighted a single home-dipped candle which she stuck onto a spike in a support post. "See?"

"Yes." I could not help adding, "A lantern would be safer." And it would have been, for nothing burns so fast or easily as a barn.

"Lanterns come dear an' burn boughten oil," she corrected me. "These don't cost an' give as good a light."

I could have argued the point but did not. I began to strip my few things from the yellow.

"I'll tend to him," she said.

"It's all right," I told her.

"Please, no. Poppa told me to tend them." What she said was ordinary enough, I suppose, but there was an urgency in her voice that came close to being a sound of fear.

"Is that so important?"

"Yes, sir. It is." Again ordinary words, but fearfully delivered.

I stepped back from the yellow and said, "I wouldn't want to cause you trouble.

"Thank you, sir." She sounded terribly grateful.

I watched her remove the gear and give each horse a skillful and thorough rubdown. I could have no complaint with the way she handled them. To break the silence I asked, "Your name is Emmy, isn't it?"

"Yes, sir. Short for Emily." She took a soft dandy-brush and began working on the buckskin's coat. She could not know that the yellow was the important one of the two.

"You're the oldest of the family, I take it."

She hesitated. The brush began to move again without her looking my way. "Now," she said.

"Meaning?"

She shrugged, still looking only at the buckskin's well-brushed flank. "There's two older. Both boys. They run off a while back. But like I said . . . they're boys."

"I hope they bettered themselves," I said in an attempt to be polite.

"They did."

"You've heard from them then."

"Nope." She replaced the brush carefully to its place on the wall and fetched two generous measures of grain. She again refused my help and carried in water for both horses. Even by the feeble light of the one candle I could see that the stalls were as clean inside as many houses I have known.

"Thank you," I said.

"You're welcome, sir." She dropped into an odd little curtsy. For the first time then she allowed her eyes to meet mine. She gave me a tiny smile and said, "Lord, it must be grand to be rich."

I thought about denying that but did not. I felt rich and no doubt looked it in my fine suit and tall boots and a brand new beaver-felt hat. I smiled back at her and walked toward the house, the girl following at a respectful distance to the rear.

# CHAPTER 18

I have ever been good at getting and enjoying my sleep—which fact seems always to surprise wide-eyed boys and excitable young ladies who have read too often the fiction that scouts and gunfighters, or at least I, sleep in a manner other than that of ordinary men—but that night at the Carlston farm I was awakened at some time well before dawn.

My senses were dulled by the depth of my slumber, else I would not have made the mistake, but at first I assumed I had been wakened by the family hound intruding himself beneath my covers. I paid no great attention to this and began to drift back away.

I seemed to dream then about a silken presence wanton beside me, and I responded as a man will. It was some minutes later, somewhat too late if you will, that I realized this was no dream and that young Emily was neither so very young nor so very skinny as I had thought. The interlude lingered enjoyably long, and I thanked her warmly when she found it necessary to depart, prior to her parents' normal waking hour. They the meanwhile had been asleep in the loft above.

I had had but little sleep yet was of robust appetite at the breakfast table, which I shared with the family. The table was well filled with meats and fresh eggs, and from the smaller child's reaction I gathered that this was a rarity. Emily paid scant attention to me during the course of the meal, but the little girl, whose name was Rosalie, more than made up for this with a stream of questions and bright-bubbling comments that even her father's dour presence could not quell. The breakfast-time treat seemed to have started her day with a holiday air.

Later, during the washing up, while I sat enjoying my coffee, I noticed Emily in whispered conversation with her younger sister. After that the child's mood was glum, and soon thereafter Emily disappeared from the house.

Someone had already tended to my horses before I ventured outside, so it was with pleasure that I retrieved them and handed Carlston a shining half eagle. I mounted the buckskin and took him and the good yellow down the road.

I had not gone two miles when a young woman stepped out into my path. I was quite near her before I realized that she was Emily Carlston.

She was dressed not in the loose sacking I had seen earlier, but in a proper if somewhat plain dress a size or two too large for her. Her hair was neatly pinned and was covered by a prim bonnet. She bore nothing in her hands.

"You make a pretty sight in the road there," I told her.

"Thank you, sir." She seemed quite shy now, although she had not been so a few hours earlier.

"Is there something I can do for you, Emily?"

At this innocent question she looked quite stricken. Her face went pale and her fingers went to her throat. I could see that she was trembling. "Please, sir. I can't go back now."

"What do you mean by that?"

"This is my mama's church dress and bonnet. And by now my father will know. They'll have seen the stains on the linen. I can't go back there now. There was . . . another brother. Younger than me. Poppa got mad after Billy an' Leon run off. He hit Jimmy with the hoe handle. Too hard. Busted something inside him. He died a couple days after an' got buried up on the knoll. If I go back I'll get it worse than him."

"I see."

"Please, sir. I *got* to go with you. An' I won't trouble you any or ever be wasteful. I swear."

I looked at her and did not know what to do with her. I could well believe her story about Carlston and did not wish to send her back into his hands. "Does your mother know about this?"

She shook her head. "She'da told Poppa. She ain't hateful or anything like that, mind, but she wouldn't ever cross him. She's got troubles enough without that. I did tell Rosie good-bye. I couldn't leave without that. But I knowed I couldn't ask you to carry her along too. And she's always been the baby of the family. She shouldn't get it too awful bad for me going."

I really had no choice in the matter without being unduly cruel to a girl who had been kind to me. And she was quite delightful in her own way.

"I'll switch my saddle to the yellow," I told her. "You can ride on the buckskin if you like."

"Thank you, sir." The relief was evident in her expression, quickly followed by fear. "Poppa might come after us. He'll be mad at you too if he does."

"That might not be a bad thing," I said, thinking it could solve a problem for her and for her sister as well as for myself—for already I was wondering if she would become a burden—but Carlston did not appear and I did not choose to ride back and seek him out, by nature being one to refrain from violence and to avoid legal warrants whenever possible. In fact, I took the precaution of turning south toward Arkansas so as to avoid trouble here.

I would like to point out that I did not in any way seek to entice the girl away from her family, made to her no promises (nor were any asked) and allowed her to accompany me at her own pleading. She asked but one question before we left that place.

"Sir?"

"Yes?"

"If you don't mind, sir . . . what is your name?"

The question struck me as a funny one and so I was in a good humor when I led Emily Carlston south into Arkansas.

# CHAPTER 19

Expenses came heavier with the girl in tow. My "packhorse" game was temporarily ruined, so I had to buy another saddle horse. And a sidesaddle for Emily. And some dresses and such. Before long the yellow really was having to carry a pack just so we could get around.

There were always fools available with more money than judgment, though, so it did not take too long to build my stash back into a comfortable bulge in my pocket. And I certainly am not complaining about the girl's insistence on traveling with me. She was a pleasant-mannered little thing and did her best to see that I was comfortable and happy.

If I were going to fault her it would have to be in the area of handling money. Lord, but that child was tightfisted. She thought it was just fine to bring the money in, but she just naturally hated to lay any down for the other half of a wager. And she did fuss some when I would set the losers up to a round of drinks so that we could leave a place without worrying about what the people were saying and doing behind our backs. After a month or so of good behavior she began to get snippy about it, and I decided it was time I put a halt to that.

"You must of spent five dollars pouring likker into those dumb farm boys this afternoon," she said to me one evening. "I've told you and told you you shouldn't do that. We could use that money our ownselves, sweetheart. You oughtn't to be so free with it as you are."

Well, I had been expecting something of that sort, and I was ready for her. I wheeled around from the mirror where

I'd been shaving—which I was having to do nearly every day by now—and gave her a long stare.

"It cost me seven dollars if you want to know," I told her coldly, "out of sixty-eight dollars I made today. Which will set *you* up to your comforts for a couple more weeks, and you might want to think on *that* part of it too." I snorted some.

"Just step back and take a look at the person who is doing that complaining, girl. Just take a look at yourself. It wasn't so very long ago you were a ragtag farmer's kid yourself, you know. You had to steal from your own mama to have a dress fit to be seen in public in.

"Now you're sitting there perched on the edge of a featherbed in the best hotel in this burg, wearing a blue silk dress and button-up shoes the like of which you never would have *seen* if I hadn't come along. You sit mighty proud on that brown mare I bought for you, and you ride a sidesaddle like a lady would. You haven't gone hungry a day since I took you in, nor been beat on or even strapped, which is not to say that I shouldn't give you some licks for the way you've been acting lately. Every stitch on your back comes from me in just the same way as I bought those drinks. Because I damn well chose to do the buying.

"Now if you aren't satisfied, girl, just you up and walk away. Any time you want. I got no hold on you. I won't try to stop you. You can even keep the clothes I bought you. Is that what you want, Em? Is it now?"

Well, that hit the mark where it was supposed to. Her face got white and her eyes flooded up and spilled over. The next thing you know she was down on her knees in that pretty silk dress, bawling and clutching at my feet and promising she would never again nag at me or interfere in my rightful business and begging that I not send her away.

"I won't this time, but mind your tongue in the future, girl. Now let go of my feet and wash your face. You look too much of a mess for me to be interested in. And while you're doing that I am going down to visit with my friends and set them up to some drinks if I damn well feel like it."

It was pleasing to see how quickly she hurried to comply, and she never said a word of complaint when I wiped the lather away and pulled my coat on and headed down the hotel stairs.

She needed the lesson, so I gave her a good one and had a roistering fine time with the boys I found in a nearby hog-wallow. It was near dawn when I got back to the hotel, whipped down and worn out and smelling strong of French perfume and sweat. She was wide awake and waiting for me, all smiles and sweetness and apologies, so I believed it to have been a lesson well taught.

All of which is to show that Miss Emily was not the sweet and innocent thing she is lately pictured to have been. She was more greedy and nagging than sweet and innocent, but I did my best to correct her from the error of her ways.

For a time, then, things went all right. I used up much of Arkansas and went back into Missouri, where as far as I knew there were no warrants out for me or for the girl.

The yellow horse and I were not unknown any longer, though, and people had heard of the fast-running "pack-horse" wherever we went. It got to the point where I quit trying to play that game and put my saddle back on the yellow where it belonged.

It was getting harder to match races for the yellow, and I had to start giving odds before I could get a run for him.

That cut down a considerable amount on the money I could expect to take in whenever I did make a match for him, and Emily began her nagging again. I began to wish I had old Jon Keene's skill at disguising an animal to look like another.

There came a time, too, when some fellow ran a ringer in on me, a regular racing horse that he suckered me into running on a short track, and that night I was the one who was being bought drinks for instead of the other way around.

Emily chose that night to begin her nagging again and to try to up the ante when she thought I was down.

"Jason. Please. You've got to listen to me, honey. We're near about broke. The whole world seems to know about that yellow horse an' the poor thing's been run half to death anyway trying to keep money in your pocket, honey. He's about used up even if you could find people to run against him, which you can't anymore." She was getting that scared, teary-eyed look about her which she was trying to use on me more and more of late and which I was coming to despise.

"Please listen to me, honey. God knows I love you, Jason. I've proved that over and over every day. I've given you everything of myself and done everything you ever asked of me. Please, honey, do something for me this time. *Please* let's settle down now. Give up this gambling and running horses and being on the road all the time. We have enough left we could rent a little house. You could find a good job. You're bright, Jason, and you're quick. People like you. Anyone would want you. We'd do real good, honey, an' you know I'll make you a good wife. You said we'd get married someday anyhow. Now would be a real good time for that. It'd work out good, honey, I promise."

That last part, about me marrying her, proved that she really thought she had me down and weak. She was trying to throw back on me as serious the kind of things a man will say to a woman when he is sweet-talking her and should not be held accountable for them come the light of day.

She should have known better, but she went on and on like that until she passed the limits of my endurance and the only way to shut her up, for her own good and for mine, was to box her ears for her. Which I did, although even under duress I was careful that I should not shame her by leaving marks on her where any might show.

The next day she did not feel up to traveling, so I went down to a late breakfast alone. I chanced there to see the owner of the racing horse which the day before had bested my yellow. He had introduced himself as Asa Purcell. He seemed in quite a good humor and joined me at my table.

"Ready to run again today?" he asked lightly.

"Not at that short distance," I told him. "My horse is no sprinter and I never should have agreed to run him at half a mile. So in answer to your question, Mr. Purcell, I must decline."

"All right then. A proper test if you like. Two miles, say? The same two runners. Each rested overnight."

That sounded better, and I had to be interested. The good yellow had never been bested on a run of two miles or greater. But I had at that time only eleven dollars left in my purse. I knew I could not run today for that amount when just yesterday I had paid out several hundred, most of it to this man.

"I am afraid I must decline, sir."

"Oh, come now, Mr. Evers. You are a sporting man. And you say your horse is the faster at the distance."

"I remember saying no such thing. The only way to prove which is the faster is to run them. I say only that my horse is not a sprinter but a distance runner."

"You do believe, though, that yours is the better."

"I do."

"And I feel that mine is. I think it would be interesting to learn which of us is correct."

"Again, Mr. Purcell, I must decline. To be quite frank with you, I haven't the cash to post a reasonable stake for the race."

"That is truly a shame." He seemed willing to drop the matter then. He drank a cup of coffee with me and we talked of unimportant things. Somewhere in the conversation he commented on "the lovely young lady you are traveling with." I agreed that she was.

"Your wife?" he asked.

I might normally have protected her pride by lying for her, but on this morning I was still irked with her over her behavior the previous night. "No," I told him. "Just a . . . friend."

Purcell smiled. "I envy your . . . friendship."

We talked a little longer and he returned to the subject of a match race.

"You believe in your horse, Mr. Evers, and I believe in mine. Would five hundred dollars tempt you?"

"It would, Mr. Purcell, if I had five hundred to wager. I already told you that I do not."

"So you did. But what about my five hundred against something of yours that I would consider of equal value?"

"The only thing I own of that value is the yellow. I would not stake him, I assure you."

"Quite frankly, Mr. Evers, I think neither of us would want to own the loser of the race. Only the winner. Yes?"

I nodded.

"You might think my suggestion . . . unusual," he went on, "but I think you might have something to wager against my five hundred cash."

"I wouldn't know what."

"I would be willing to stake five hundred dollars in gold coin against your, uh, interest in your . . . friend."

Purcell pulled a heavy purse from his pocket and laid down the money in five small, neat stacks of twenties. Those coins could give me months of worry-free living and more than enough time to give the yellow the rest he truly needed.

"I cannot wager what I don't own, Mr. Purcell."

"I understand that, Mr. Evers. You stake only your interest in the, uh, matter." He smiled. "I believe I am capable of mastering the situation thereafter." The smile became broader. "If, of course, I am right about my horse. If I am not, of course, you recoup your losses and quite a bit more."

Purcell drained the last of his coffee and stood. "Think it over, Mr. Evers. I plan to have lunch at the hotel here. About noon or soon after. We can discuss it again then if you wish." He smiled. "Have a pleasant morning, sir."

# CHAPTER 20

The truth is that Emily had been right; I had been running the yellow hard and often of late and he was not in the shape he should have been in. I had been telling myself that he was in racing trim, but in fact he had gotten plain underweight and gaunted.

I could see that now, as I groomed and saddled him, and I must admit to some regrets that I had found Purcell at his dinner and accepted the man's wager. I would not have done that if I had first gone around to the barn and given the yellow horse a critical inspection.

Nor had I known about the running in time to have the stableboy withhold water from him at the morning feeding so that he could make his run light in the belly. Still, Purcell had not known about it either, so the race should be a fair one on that count.

And we were running at two miles. I kept reminding myself of that. Purcell's horse was a sprinter. He could be expected to beat me at three-quarters of a mile and perhaps for the first full mile. Beyond that my yellow should best him. This was not another sprint.

I set the saddle carefully into place and cinched it only tight enough that it should not shift on the one hard turn we would make, but not so tight that it would interfere with the horse's motion. I washed his legs and checked his feet with care.

As always, the good horse seemed near sleep when I led him out and mounted him.

This was no public race, but a contest between two

horses and two men. There were no crowds waiting for us, only Purcell with his horse and young rider, a man grown but even shorter and lighter of body than I. They waited at the pole we would use for the start and finish line, and Purcell stayed there alone while his rider and I rode out to inspect the turnaround pole.

I did not greatly care for the road we were to run. There were patches of melting snow along it and bogs of slick mud we would have to cross. Still, both horses had to run the same course, and at least there was no ice. It would have to do.

We returned to the start, and a few curious onlookers had gathered beside Purcell.

"Shall I signal the start, or would you rather one of these gentlemen did the honor?" Purcell asked.

"Go ahead," I said. I nudged the yellow up to the line and noticed as I did so that Purcell's sleek sprinter today was quiet and controlled on the line. His horse was a dark sorrel, and the gleam of health in its coat made it look like a bronze casting in the sunlight.

"Settle your horses then, gentlemen," Purcell said. "You may break on the count of three."

He made the count loudly in a slow-measured cadence, and I spurred the yellow forward.

The sorrel leaped ahead of us, but not so jackrabbit quick as he had the day before. The rider was holding some of his strength in reserve for this longer run, and the tactic seemed to anger the yellow. Clods of cold mud flew up from the sorrel's hooves to rain down onto the yellow and onto me.

We drove past the half-mile post that had marked our finish yesterday, and the yellow was still reaching for the rhythm of his great, flowing speed. Still the sorrel hung just before us.

At three quarters we began to gain, but the sorrel was

still stretching out as well. The wind was cold and noisy across my ears.

The sorrel went wide at the turn, but rounded it fairly. The yellow cut closer to the mark and we closed the distance somewhat. I could see Purcell's rider turning to see that we rounded the marker as we should, and he gave me a curt nod when he saw that we did so.

We held close like that for the next half mile, the sorrel little more than a length ahead of us. By stretching and reaching I might have grabbed the tail streaming out so tantalizingly near.

We thundered across the mud patches and I had to turn my head and press my face down close to the yellow's mane to avoid the pelting clods. The yellow gained ground until his head was beside the sorrel's flank.

Both horses were stretching now, nostrils wide and reaching into the wind, the sound of their breathing a harsh undertone to the thud of their hooves.

The sorrel seemed to slip and falter on the muddy footing. It was ever so slight, but of a sudden we were beside him.

I looked into the face of Purcell's rider and he was grim. I do not doubt that my own expression was just as grim.

We had less than a quarter to go now and were running stride for stride.

The ending post flashed nearer, and I spurred the yellow hard, raking him as I never had before. Out of the corner of my eye I could see the rise and fall of the other rider's hand as he went to the whip.

The gallant yellow's stride held, but he had no more to give me. He was already giving it all.

Under the whip the sorrel turned loose of what little he still had, and he began to edge forward until my head was beside the rider's boots and then the sweat-dark sorrel flank and finally his croup.

And it was there we finished, bested by half a length. I sat upright on the weary yellow, the taste of mud and defeat in my mouth, and let him slow before I returned to the starting pole.

I must give Purcell his credit. When I slid to the ground beside him, his smile was one of welcome and admiration rather than gloating victory. He pumped my hand.

"By God, Evers, that was a race of races, sir. I'd have been as proud to lose it as I am to win it. It was a privilege just to have seen them run. Why, my horse is considered a champion on the other side of the river yet yours, in poor condition and full fed this morning, came within half a stride of beating him."

"You checked his feeding?" I asked somewhat stupidly. I suppose I was still somewhat shocked at the loss.

"Of course. Before I spoke with you earlier." He shook his head admiringly. "My champion could not have run so well on feed. Really."

Purcell gripped my shoulder and said, "Mr. Evers, I am not a man to go back on a wager, but I beg of you. Let me buy this horse. Call the five hundred I staked a part of that and let me buy him. We could call off the debt and you keep the five hundred in cash besides. Would you do that, sir?"

I looked at the tired, shivering yellow, so homely but so game, and I could not. I shook my head.

Purcell sighed. "I can't blame you. If I owned him I could not part with him either. But, my, how he would do in Kentucky." He stroked the yellow's muzzle with what looked to be regret. "You, boy," he said to a nearby youngster. "Walk this horse down. Don't bring him back until he's cool. He deserves good treatment."

The youngster led the yellow away—I would have to give the boy at least a dime when he returned—and Purcell and I slipped away from the crowd that had gathered around our horses. Purcell was all business now.

"How do you want to, uh, make the transfer, Evers?"

"I hadn't really thought about that."

"No? I have a suggestion then."

"Make it."

"We can make this the easiest on all concerned if you like."

"I would," I assured him.

"Then give me your room key. No more than that. You will be leaving the town?"

"Yes. And Missouri, I think."

"Of course. I'll have your things delivered to you at the livery then. And good luck to you."

I gave him the key, and that was that.

I do wish to state here, though, that it is totally untrue that I delivered Emily Carlston into a life of ill repute. I have neither knowledge of nor involvement in her activities after we parted, and I cannot be held accountable for whatever her actions have been. I did no more than allow Asa Purcell to petition her as man to woman, and it would not have been right of me to deny her an opportunity to enjoy the companionship of a wealthy man, which had been—and, I assume, still was—her fondest goal. I had given her help when she asked it of me those months before when she begged to leave her father's home, and I had treated her kindly since that time. I made no promises to her that went unfulfilled, and my actions throughout our friendship were blameless despite the ugly tales to the contrary. Nor, as I have described, was she the innocent she lately has been made out to be. To this I do attest here and now, and I would defy those who say otherwise to prove their vicious falsehoods. This they cannot do.

# CHAPTER 21

In many ways it was quite comfortable to again be traveling in solitude, and I was not wholly without assets when I left that place. I still had eleven dollars in cash and was soon able to dispose of the now unnecessary sidesaddle for twenty dollars and of the surplus brown mare for forty-five.

My expenses were small, as I purchased a few foodstuffs and lay out in the woods for a time while the yellow recouped his strength and I took the time to think toward the future.

The yellow horse was still my greatest asset, I concluded, as it was only hard use and low condition that had led to his recent defeat. Furthermore, I could now take advantage of the word-of-mouth news that he had been bested. The southwestern Missouri farmers would again be willing to lay their money against him. After a few weeks of rest I should be able to resume a comfortable life by way of his unfailing speed.

In order to do this, though, I felt it best to remain in closely settled Missouri, where I had enjoyed such success in the past. In hindsight I wish now that I had turned then toward Kansas as had been my intention.

After the horse was sufficiently rested I matched him in a few penny-ante races which were of no consequence but which did enable me to again build my stake to a respectable level, without which I could not hope to compete for earnings of any appreciable amount.

On the morning of the eleventh day of June, 1868, I entered a small town, the name of which I did not know, as no signs were posted at the town limits.

While normally I would have sought out a hotel bar or local saloon to make my match, I this time strayed from custom when I saw a group of men gathered near the loading dock of a mercantile. There were eight or nine gathered there and they seemed to be admiring a bright red saddle horse held by one of their number.

The horse was of a fancy grade, fine-boned and handsome in appearance. He had a reputation for speed to match his racy appearance. This I knew quite well, as I had twice bested him down in Arkansas not three months earlier. At that time he had been able to outpull my yellow for the first half mile, was even at three-quarters and had faded far to the rear by the mile post. I had run him then at something like a mile and a half, and neither race had been a contest.

The situation at hand seemed ready-made for me to fill out my poke and be able again to lay high stakes. I turned my buckskin and the pack-laden yellow toward the men.

"Handsome animal you have there," I said by way of greeting as I neared them.

"He is," agreed the man holding the reins.

"Looks fast."

"He is that too."

"Faster than my old packhorse, do you think?"

The man snorted his disgust and would have turned away, but another fellow with similar dark, unkempt hair and pale brown or tan eyes—they seemed to bear a family resemblance, I saw at once—leaned close to him and whispered into his ear.

The horse holder grinned and said, "Danny tells me your packhorse is a ringer and fast. He says you pay in cash when you lose a race. Like you done not too awful long ago."

I shrugged. "Nobody wins every time."

"My horse is a champion down to Arkansas where I bought him."

"I like to think that mine is a strong runner up on this side of the line," I told him.

"Light down," the man invited, "an' maybe we can work out a way to see which is the faster."

"Maybe we can at that."

I stepped down from the buckskin and spent some time loosening his cinch so the farmer would have ample time to take in the unlikely appearance of my good yellow.

The man introduced himself as Leon Baker and his brother as Daniel. Leon was the owner of the red runner and had taken delivery of it only the night before.

"This could be my chance to get back a part of my cost," he said.

"Or lose it," I suggested.

Leon seemed to find that quite amusing. He laughed right heartily and said, "There's no tricks here about yours being a packhorse, Evers. This time you face a straight-up racer, by damn."

"You still have to win before you take my money. What odds do you offer?"

"Horse for horse and dollar for dollar, by damn."

"You don't mean by that to wager the horse too, do you?" I asked. In truth I did not want the flashy-looking red, for he did not run nearly as well as he looked.

"No, because I wouldn't have that scrawny yellow thing in my barn. I'll go you even money on it, though."

"All right," I said. "Would you say two miles would be a fair test?"

Daniel again whispered in his brother's ear, and I was guessing that he would be telling more about what he had heard of my run with Purcell. They would know that the yellow had come close to beating Purcell at that distance.

"The red was just delivered," Baker said, "and I don't know his condition yet. I'll run you at a mile, though." He seemed to believe he had me hung up and cooling like a butchered shoat.

"I'll split it with you. A mile and a half," I said.

Baker looked at his brother and got back a short, barely seen negative shake of the head. He seemed to think that over for a moment but gave in to his greed. He did not want to see me walk away.

"A mile and a half, then. And a straight run. No turns. Start out on the road an' finish here in town where everyone can see. Fair enough?"

"It sounds fair to me, Mr. Baker."

Baker's pals were starting to get excited about it too. They began talking and wanting in on the money.

"I'll put up"—he dug into his pocket—"three hundred of my own," Baker said. His friends were trying to offer ten- and twenty-dollar bets.

"Hold on, gentlemen," I told them. "I can't cover you all, but I'll stake what I have." I reached into my pocket and laid my purse out for them to see. I let them count it out to be two hundred sixty-two dollars. "That is what I can wager."

Now the truth is that I had learned by now to hold out a small reserve against emergency use, so the amount in my purse was what I had been willing to stake before I ever rode into this town and became aware of the windfall of the red gelding.

Baker and his friends argued somewhat over the distribution of my poke and seemed not to care that I was listening to their greed. In the end Baker took two hundred, his brother put up twenty and the remainder was divided up among their friends. They added their money to mine, the poke was set atop a post and it was agreed that no one should approach it but the winner of the race. It was also agreed that Daniel would be our starter.

I transferred my saddle to the yellow and waited patiently while Baker prepared his animal. His rider was a boy who might have been his son or perhaps just a youngster from the town. The finish was to be the post where the winnings lay.

The bettors waited near the post while Daniel and the boy and I rode out on the road from town to a distance that I judged nearer a mile and a quarter than a mile and a half. I chose not to argue with him about his petty little attempt to cheat me. It should be obvious from this that I did everything in my power to be agreeable and aboveboard.

As for the race itself, I could not honestly say there was anything greatly exciting about it. In fact, the red runner *did* seem tired and out of shape from his delivery north into Missouri. The yellow was even with him before the half mile, and at the finish I had ample time to slow the yellow and swing him near the post where the winner's stakes waited. I plucked the bag off the post and had turned back toward the crowd before the red crossed the line.

"My treat, boys, if you'd like a beer," I offered.

Baker was black-faced with anger, but he said nothing and tried to put up a good appearance before his friends. He followed the crowd to a two-story inn, where I tied the yellow outside and went in to set them up to a few dollars worth of salve for injured pride.

They were all scarcely into their first beer and I into a mug of strong coffee when a slightly built, tow-headed young man came down the stairs and, upon seeing me, immediately made his way through the group to where I stood.

"Mr. Evers," he said with a smile and a nod, "it's nice to see you again."

I said hello and realized that I had seen him somewhere before, but could not remember where or when.

"You know this man, Ernie?" Leon Baker demanded.

"Oh sure, Mr. Baker. Him and my dad matched a couple races down home this winter. I rode against him twice."

Now, too late, it came back to me.

Ernie Lefler chuckled. "As a matter of fact, Mr. Baker, Mr. Evers here and that yella horse of his are the biggest reason my father decided to sell his runnin' horse. I guess you wouldn't have yourself a good runner today if it wasn't for him. Dad just didn't have the heart to keep feeding the red after Mr. Evers's ugly ol' yellow beat him so bad."

Baker looked absolutely fit to burst, and I took a step or two away to make sure I would have plenty of room to bring my .44 into use.

The man glared at me and at the revolver in my waistband and spun around without a word. He was stiff-legged with fury as he walked out of the inn.

I thought that that was that and concluded that the best thing I could do now would be to put some miles behind me. I was just starting toward the street when I heard a gunshot outside and the fall of a heavy body. I wondered if Baker might have shot himself. The truth did not occur to me.

I stepped onto the plank sidewalk, more curious than anything else, and was greeted by the most awful sight I have ever seen. My yellow horse was down in the dirt of the street with the blood seeping from his head. Leon Baker was walking away from him.

I moved aside so my back would not be exposed in the doorway, took careful aim and dropped Baker with a single bullet to the back of the head. It was as humane a shot as he had used on my good horse.

Daniel Baker stepped out onto the sidewalk beside me. His features clouded with the same unreasoning fury I had so recently seen on his brother's face and I shot once into his body, the bullet entering his left side and coursing through his organs.

People who were not there at the time have since claimed from the calm safety of their armchairs that Daniel Baker was unarmed and presented no threat to me. They did not see the ugliness of coming murder on his face. I did.

Furthermore, I make no apologies to them nor to any other man. If I had it to do over again I would yet pull my trigger on Leon Baker and on Daniel Baker. I only wish that Leon Baker had taken as long to die as did his brother and had to suffer as much. That is my *only* regret in the matter.

It was with a heavy heart that I reclaimed my saddle from the fallen yellow horse and rode the little buckskin away from that foul community toward Kansas. Bitter experience had already proven to me that I could expect no justice from the law, and so there would undoubtedly be warrants issued against me in Missouri.

I felt quite alone again without the patient yellow horse's muzzle bobbing close to my knee.

# CHAPTER 22

Abilene in early summer was a completely different place from Abilene in late fall. The first few herds of the season were beginning to come in and already the buyers were crowing about their good prospects for the year—unless of course there were Texas cowmen within hearing, in which case the buyers would bemoan the state of the market, the state of the cattle and the state of their rising expenses.

Abilene before had been a quiet and gentlemanly sort of town, at least in its own way, but now it was lusty and brawling. The streets were busy night and day and all of the vices were delightfully available.

There were a number of men in town who remembered me—Ronald Sepin not among them this season—and I quickly regained an enjoyment of the popularity I had known here before.

The bow-legged and saddlesore drovers, wild though they often were, walked wide around me when I passed. They had heard of Jason Evers and knew not to quarrel with the .44 behind my belt. They shot or cut each other, but left me alone.

The single exchange I had with any of their kind was once as I was passing one of the dime-a-dance halls and two very drunken, big-hatted boys came stumbling out.

The one in the lead happened to bump into me, to which I took no offense. He, however, became quite excited. The boy—I use the term boy here even though he was probably several years my senior by a calendar count—mouthed a series of derogatory oaths and demanded that I apologize or "be blown two ways to Christmas an' twice on Sunday." This seemed to him to make some sort of sense and to be threatening as well.

"Take your friend and go away," I told the other one, "or I'll hang him up to cool like so much beef brought up here for slaughter."

I fingered the butt of the Colt Army at my belly and the second boy's eyes widened. "C'mon, Jim. We got to get back to the herd."

"Not 'til this sonuvabitch apologizes," Jim said. He was a sawed-off and ugly little wart with arms too long for his body, and I suppose I should have gotten angry, but I did not.

"Take him home and maybe he'll grow up to be something someday," I told his buddy. "But if he keeps after me I'll have to kill him."

"C'mon, Jim, for Christ's sake. That's Jason Evers you're sassing. He could eat you an' me both for breakfast an' use our bones to pick his teeth. Now come *on*." The more sober of the two gave me an apologetic sort of grin and pulled his friend away by the elbow.

An incident like that might well have made another man mad, but I was not. Which should, I think, demonstrate the evenness of my temper at this as at most times. I have never been one to act rashly, as I think all who know the facts must agree.

Abilene was, as before, good to me, and I enjoyed my return to a comfortable style of living. I took a suite of rooms at the KC House, which had been built, furnished and staffed during my absence, and I seldom lacked for company.

Naturally I felt certain obligations to my friends and, while the society in which I moved was stimulating to the mind and the senses, it was nonetheless draining on the purse. The money with which I had arrived in town began to fade away. I regretted not a penny of it and at the time gave it little thought.

There came the night, though, when I did not have the cash to cover my bets at the gaming tables and was required to sign a marker for what was lacking. I ended the evening with several notes outstanding.

The following morning I was awakened somewhat before my usual hour by a polite rapping on my door. I responded cautiously, dressed with the little .32 if not with my britches, and answered the knock. A rather distinguished-looking man waited in the hallway.

"Do you remember me, Mr. Evers?"

"Of course. Clark Jamison, right? As I recall, you were the big winner at last night's game. Come in."

He did, dropping his round hat onto a nearby table and making himself comfortable in my sitting room.

Jamison was a head taller than I and portly of build. He gave a strong impression of power and money combined in a most respectable whole. Even at that early hour he looked freshly shaved and impeccably groomed.

I felt at something of a disadvantage in my drawers and so excused myself. Jamison seemed content to wait.

When I returned to the sitting room he had smoked half of a cigar, but exhibited no impatience. I thought I knew what he wanted.

"You are holding two of my markers, I believe," I said as I took a seat next to him on the settee.

"All three of them, actually," he said. He reached beneath his coat to an inside pocket and extracted the folded papers that I recognized from the night before.

Before I could explain my temporary inability to redeem them, Jamison tore the three slips in half and in half again. He handed me the now worthless scraps.

"I wouldn't want these to get in the way of a friendly business discussion," he said.

"You certainly have my attention," I told him. Which was a natural fact. He had as good as torn up that much money, which is enough to attract anyone's full attention.

"Good," he said emphatically. "You see, I am much more interested in paying you money than in collecting any from you."

I let my eyebrows rise a notch. "I already said you had my attention. Now you have my interest as well."

"*Very* good, Mr. Evers. Would you be offended if I sent down for a pot of coffee? This might take a little time."

It did. It took the pot of coffee and the rest of Jamison's long cigar before we were finished.

What he told me in essence was that he was an officer of the railroad—which railroad may become obvious, but its name will not be repeated now by me as I believe I owe them that much, all things considered; and in complete candor I may as well admit, too, that the name Jamison is a randomly chosen alias—and that he had for some time been searching for a man of my exact qualifications.

"We have checked your record quite carefully, Mr. Evers, and are prepared to have our legal staff quash indictments outstanding against you in Colorado and in Arizona territories." He held a hand up before I could offer explanation. "You don't need to proclaim your innocence. We are well aware that a man can justify his own actions. That will not be necessary. We do regret that under the present political climate we can do nothing about the charges outstanding against you in Texas. However, until or unless the Ranger companies are reactivated there, I believe you could move freely in the state anywhere outside the immediate environs of Austin itself. I would not suggest visiting the capital. Nor would it become necessary as part of your work if you should agree to our offer."

Having placed a considerable amount of sweetener into the pot, he went on to explain that the railroad was experiencing certain difficulties in securing right of way. Although government grants and construction bonuses were designed to guarantee access, there were in some places conflicting land claims filed under state and territorial grants and under homestead provisions. Resolution of these disputes through legal channels could be time-consuming and costly. Such delays would not be in the best interests of the railroad or of its stockholders. Nor, he added, would delay be in the interests of the territory the newly building railroad would eventually serve. Assistance given to the railroad would be assistance given to every resident who would someday benefit from its link to and from the nation's marketing centers. He emphasized this point quite strongly.

The railroad, he said, wanted to employ me or someone with my talents as a sub rosa agent to assist in clearing out these impediments. Although I would not be listed on their regular payroll—and would report directly to Jamison—they would be willing to pay me a standard fee of $250 per "problem solved," plus all expenses incurred in my work.

After some discussion it was further agreed, as I would need some base of operations where Jamison could locate me, that the railroad would assume the expense of permanently maintaining my suite of rooms at the KC House. This was the nearest thing I had ever had to a home of my own and pleased me greatly. They also, of course, provided me with travel passes for myself and any livestock transported for my personal use.

It was, I thought, a completely equitable and aboveboard arrangement. I shook Jamison's hand on it and accepted a one hundred dollar advance against expenses.

# CHAPTER 23

The railroad was wanting to build south and west from Kansas and avoid the high mountain passes of the old Santa Fe Trail, basically following the same route as the Cimarron Cutoff, although not precisely so.

A small portion of the proposed route touched Colorado, but it was not in conflict with any claimed lands there. More of it crossed the I.T., or Indian Territory—but, of course, the government took care of the right of way there. And Kansas itself was cooperative enough that I think the state officials would have personally booted some sod-busters' tails if any had interfered with the right of way.

The first real problem area was to be in New Mexico, the Texas panhandle being barren and unsettled enough to cause no immediate difficulties.

In New Mexico, though, there were a lot of Mexicans who had been on the land for quite a while and resisted giving the railroad permission to cross what they regarded as their own. This even though it was not the U.S. government, but the Mexicans or even the Spaniards, who had given them title. Jamison asked me to handle the problems there.

My first time out he gave me two packhorses, several cases of .44 rimfire shells and the help of a man who had been in the preliminary route-survey crew.

D. K. Bryan was a tall, skinny fellow in his mid-thirties who had learned his surveying in western Illinois and in Iowa before the war, spent the war years trying to get himself transferred from the engineers to cavalry, but could not because at 165 pounds he was too heavy, and after the war decided his best avenue to adventure and travel was in railroading.

He told me all this and much more within an hour of our meeting. I was not really interested in knowing so much about the man.

"We saw a band of wild Comanche last fall when we were running the grades down into Texas. They weren't any blanket Indians either. You could tell. We'd brought a couple cases of government surplus Spencers with us, and we passed them around and were ready, but the Comanch' never tried us. They stood off and watched us for nearly three hours, then the next thing you knew they were gone. Just like that. I don't think there was time to blink your eyes and they were gone. Nothing there but a little dust hanging in the air. We didn't see them again."

He sounded disappointed. His traveling gear, which he had hauled with him up to my suite, included a saddle scabbard that showed the butt of either a Henry or of one of the sturdier 1866 Winchester rifles like mine was. It sounded like he was willing to use the thing, whichever it was. I did not really like that about him either. The nature of my business was supposed to be strictly between Jamison and me. D. K. Bryan was not part of our agreement.

"Just what is it you're supposed to do for me, Mr. Bryan?"

He looked a little surprised. "Why, I'm supposed to help you, of course."

"No, I don't mean in general what you are supposed to do. I mean *exactly* what things were you instructed?"

"Well, my specific orders were to take you over the route we proposed last year and to show you four parcels in question down in New Mexico. And the owners' houses. I've talked with all four of them already. They would talk to me again, I'm sure."

"Were you told to negotiate with them?"

Bryan shook his head. "Not exactly, no. Just to show you to their homes. I just assumed you would want me to . . ."

"Don't," I snapped at him. "Don't be assuming more than you should." I gave him a smile and explained it for him. "Those people already know you, true, but they sent you packing last year. If you show up a second time with the same request you will probably get the same response. I'll talk to them alone, Bryan. Take a different approach with them. All you are to do is show me who it is I need to see. All right?"

He did look puzzled now. "I don't know, Mr. Evers. I mean, I'm sure Mr. Jamison knows what he's doing. And you too, of course. But I mean, you have this . . ."

"Reputation?"

Bryan smiled gratefully. "Well, yes, sir, you do. Now that's a fact, isn't it? And these people might be more intimidated than convinced unless someone introduces you and gets you started on the right foot, so to speak. And I did get along with them pretty well before. I think they'd trust me if I tell them you're all right. If you see what I mean."

"Oh, I do. Indeed I do, Bryan. And I will tell Jamison how helpful you've been. But really he does know what he is doing. I want you to trust his judgment and not do anything without checking with me first. Will you promise me that?"

"Yes, sir," he said respectfully, although he was nearly twice my age. Not that he knew it, but it was so. That was one nice thing about Abilene. They knew Jason Evers there, and they respected me.

I collected my buckskin from the public stable—still feeling the loss of my old yellow horse, if the truth be known—and turned the packhorses over to Bryan's care.

The railroad carried us to end-of-track on the work cars. We drew supplies from the company stores there and rode ahead on the prepared grade and soon beyond it. Bryan seemed quite familiar with the whole operation.

The first night we camped with a survey marking crew, most of them men Bryan had worked with in the past. Thereafter we were on our own.

We passed Fort Dodge and the encampment beyond it that had started out as a hogwallow for the garrison troops and was now becoming a center for the teams of hide hunters who made their living from the buffalo herds.

Bryan was vocal on that as on all other subjects. He said he had seen enough of the herds on his surveying journeys to know that a man could make a fine career for himself for life just by following one or two of the herds. He said he had thought about going into that business himself, as the supply of hides was inexhaustible, but he did not like the heavy labor involved in skinning and scraping. It was a dirty and foul-smelling business, he said.

Personally, I would not know. All the tales to the contrary, I myself have seen rather few buffalo on the plains, and none of them in the prairie-blackening numbers other travelers like to talk about.

Bryan led our little four-horse cavalcade across the grass without hesitation and with no visible landmarks that I could find, yet several times each day we would pass a short stake which he and the rest of the preliminary crew had placed the year before. He used his compass but little, yet never seemed to be lost. How he managed this was an amazement to me, but seemed quite natural to him.

It took us some weeks of travel in this manner before we reached what Bryan said was New Mexico, and another day until we reached the first of the problem *rancheras*.

I spent several more days in Bryan's company scouting the four locations and then dismissed the man, instructing him to return to Abilene and tell Jamison that I would not be long in following behind him.

"Look here, Jason," he said, the length of time we had spent together leading to a familiarity he would not have attempted in town, "I know you and Mr. Jamison think you know what you're about, but this country out here just isn't the same as it might seem from the comfort of a desk and chair back there in Kansas. People out here aren't always as hospitable as they're made out to be. They're suspicious too, an' sometimes with good reason. You go riding in on them cold an' you could get yourself in trouble, Jason. Let me come with you and break the ice for you."

"Bryan, I told you already what you're to do. Now take that second packhorse and go do it."

"I still don't see why I can't stop in at Santa Fe before I go back, Jason. It sure is closer than Kansas an' we've been out for a while."

"I told you already, dammit. Jamison wants to know right away, and it will sure be quicker for you to go straight back the way we came. Now don't argue with me. *Do* it."

He sighed loudly, but gave in. Which was lucky for him. When Jamison said he wanted things done in secret I was sure he meant it, and there was no need for anyone else to know that the railroad had had negotiators in the area. Public knowledge could come later, but not until I had had my chance to discuss things with the Mexican ranchers.

We split the supplies we had remaining, and Bryan left the next morning, riding back the way we had come.

# CHAPTER 24

I ran into D. K. Bryan again about a month later in a comfortable little brothel in Abilene—not one of the hog pens frequented by the cattle drovers, but an exclusive little place not known to just everyone. My purse was pleasantly heavy and I was having a glass of rather dry port and playing a game of checkers with a young lady named Charlotte.

"I heard you were back in town, Evers," he said by way of a greeting. I waved him into a vacant chair at our table.

"Yes, I got back a few days ago. Care for a glass of wine?"

Bryan shook his head. He already had a tumbler of whiskey in his hand, so I hadn't really expected him to accept. He took a drink from it and seemed to be reflecting on something. There was a look in his eyes that seemed to be asking questions.

"What is it, man?"

He glanced at Charlotte. She was a nice girl and a sensitive one. She caught his look and excused herself from the table. "I'll be back in a minute, love. Promise you won't start without me." She left in the direction of the privy.

"All right, Bryan. What is it?" I asked him a bit sharply. I had not greatly liked the man when I had to be with him. His intrusion now was even more annoying.

"I heard some talk in the office yesterday," he said. "Our Santa Fe attorneys are negotiating with those four New Mexican families for the right-of-way permissions."

"So?"

"I thought that was your job."

I shrugged. "It turned out to be just a matter of routine. I didn't have to get involved. So the lawyers are handling it. They'd have to draw the legal papers anyway."

"I heard they're dealing with four widows down there."

"That's right," I told him. "Their husbands died since you were there last year. The widows were willing to grant the easements. That is why I didn't have to get involved."

"Four men dead," he said bitterly. "Just like that. Four *good* men. Strange coincidence, don't you think?"

I took a sip of my wine and smiled at him. "Yes, I did, rather. But you told me yourself that that is rough country down there. A man just never knows, does he?"

"When did they die?"

"Some time since last fall," I told him. "Lucky thing for the railroad, wasn't it?"

He ignored that. "How?" he demanded.

"I heard they were shot. You know how those Mexicans are, though. Half of them are bandits. The rest are feuding with someone most of the time. I'm just as happy I didn't have to get involved in negotiating with them."

"They were good men," he said again.

"Yes, well, I never got acquainted with any of them. Was there something else?"

Bryan was staring at the butt of my .44. Just to twit him I scratched my stomach and let my fingers come to rest on the wooden grip.

"No," he said unhappily. "You'd never tell me what happened down there anyway. Maybe I'm better off not knowing." He took another long drink from his glass.

"What do you *think* happened, Mr. Bryan?" I was trying to tell him in a nice way, with the tone of my voice, that he should shut his mouth and change his opinions, but he either didn't hear or didn't care. Whatever caution he might have had disappeared and he answered as if my question had been a serious one.

"You're a gunman, Evers. A known killer. You even seem

to take pride in your ability at it. Well, what I think happened down there is that you used me to set those poor men up. I think you had me mark your targets for you and then you sent me away so I couldn't testify against you and then you murdered those four good men." He was getting quite excited now and his voice was beginning to rise. "Well, by God, you're just damned lucky you did send me back, because I sure God *would* have testified against you. And I still will if it ever comes to that. You can bet your last cent on that to be a fact, mister gunfighter."

He started to rise, and he moved his hand toward the .36-caliber pocket revolver I knew he always carried. I am quite, quite sure that he intended to draw his gun and shoot me down in his anger over his unfounded suspicions. I am *quite* sure of this.

Fortunately my hand was the quicker and D. K. Bryan died with a pair of .44 caliber bullets in his chest. I was greatly aggrieved that the man expired before he could make a deathbed statement to the effect that he had been trying to assassinate me.

An inquest was held before a coroner's jury impaneled in Abilene two days after the incident. I was ably represented by the law firm of Harrison, Hunter and Spurgis, who also represented the railroad's interests in the town.

Witnesses who had been present that evening testified to having heard Bryan's voice rising in an argumentative and threatening manner and that the man had been drinking heavily.

My own appearance on the stand was brief. I was sworn, I told the jurors that Bryan had attempted to murder me and I was allowed to return to my seat.

A finding of self-defense was quickly returned, and no charges were ever placed against me in the matter.

My only regret is that Bryan did not live long enough for

me to convince him of the error of his beliefs, which I would easily have been able to do had he not chosen to attack me in so unprovoked a manner. However, the guilt—and the loss—were his.

# CHAPTER 25

Jamison's helpfulness during that inquest—and through several subsequent appearances before other panels at later dates—was truly representative of the fair and honest way he always dealt with me. Although he was unable to publicly acknowledge that I was an employee of the railroad, he always saw to it that I was generously rewarded for my efforts on their behalf, and when the need arose he saw to it as well that I was always represented by the finest legal counsel available, no matter what state or territory I had been operating in.

Thanks to his unfailing assistance (I had long known better than to ascribe successes in court to any influence of truth or justice, both of which were also on my side), I never once during that period had to stand trial to answer legal charges filed against me.

Of the seven unfounded but nevertheless hotly pursued attempts to press false accusations against me, five were successfully resolved in presentations to coroner's juries, as in the Bryan matter, while the remaining two were quashed in pretrial hearings when honest judges were shown that my scurrilous accusers had evidence that was entirely insufficient for prosecution.

Details of these minor legal incidents are readily available in the public records of Kansas, New Mexico and Arizona, and I will not trouble to repeat them here.

Nor will I bother to relate the ordinary, day-to-day business dealings I undertook on behalf of the railroad during that period of approximately three years when I was employed by them in a problem-solving capacity. Such an account would be needlessly boring. It should suffice to say only that I traveled a great deal, negotiated in private with those who opposed the railroad's progress or threatened it harm and did whatever odd jobs I could to make myself a useful member of that good organization.

It is my fond belief, I might add, that during this period I was at least mildly instrumental in bringing the civilizing influence of rail commerce into the Southwest and in making rail transportation the safe and reliable form of transport it has become, free from the robbers and brigands who sometimes preyed upon the worthy and trusting passengers using other lines.

If I was able to contribute to this success I will accept that fact as its own reward and ask for no other.

I might well have remained in the employ of the railroad and sought with them a long career and an honorable retirement, except for an event that occurred on the fourth day of July in the year 1871.

I had at that time been operating again in northern New Mexico Territory. I had been working under cover, using an assumed name and trying to locate and identify the leaders of a group which was trying to subvert the free enterprise system by organizing certain of the railroad's employees. While their aims were laudatory on the surface of their arguments, the true object of this group was to economically cripple my employers so that a competing road could step in and secure right-of-way permissions already promised to Jamison and his line.

In any event, I made the necessary identifications in late June and was able to disrupt the plan. Finding myself so near a major metropolis and with the holiday approaching, I packed my rifle and few other belongings onto a mule and rode into Santa Fe in time for the celebration of our nation's birth.

Celebration of the Fourth in that city had a uniquely foreign air which was charmingly in contrast with the intent of the holiday. It was as much a fiesta celebration as an American event in that city.

During the afternoon I listened to several of the speeches offered in the principal plaza and drank iced lemonade and admired the garish costumes of the Mexican celebrants and applauded the skill of their musicians and public dance troupes. It was a gala day and a relaxing one. One might even consider it a well-earned recreation.

That evening the city was bright with lamps and hanging lanterns and well-filled candelabras, and a dance or ball might be found in nearly any hall large enough to accommodate a dozen couples or more. I dressed in my finest suit and a newly acquired low-crowned hat and resolved to look in on as many of these grand affairs as I could manage.

My intentions were forgotten immediately when I walked into the lobby of La Fonda, where I was registered.

Entering from the street at that moment was a family group consisting of a heavy-bodied gentleman whose suit pants were jammed down into the tops of high boots, a nicely dressed matron who would certainly be his wife, a young man about my own age who looked vaguely uncomfortable in high collar and tie . . . and the loveliest girl I had or have ever seen.

Her appearance then remains with me as clearly as if a photographer had been standing by with flash powder and hooded camera at the ready.

She wore a floor-length gown of a creamy ivory shade, overlaid above the waist with delicate lace and held close at the waist with a pale blue sash. A matching ribbon tied tight around a slender throat held a tiny cameo brooch just above the lace neck of her gown. Her hair was light brown and covered with a lace mantilla in the Mexican style, although there was nothing in her delicate features or clear green eyes to suggest foreign parentage.

From the first instant of viewing her I knew with absolute

certainty that she was being escorted by a brother and not by a husband or a lover, for there was about her an aura of virginal innocence that was above miscomprehension.

For some moments, before she or any of her family became aware of me across the crowded lobby, I stood frozen by my appreciation of the sight of her. Yet I have always been quick of wit, and the passage of time could not have been great. I knew at once what I had to do.

Heedless of possible consequences to my personal safety, I took the dependable .44 from its accustomed place in my waistband and shoved it out of sight beneath my coat. I turned to the nearby desk clerk and checked my years-long companion with him, a thing I had never faintly considered before that time. That could have been a dangerously foolish thing to do, but Jason Evers was well known and so was his method of carrying the big revolver that he used so well. And this lovely girl, I knew, would never consent to surrender herself into the arms of a man with the reputation of Jason Evers. Just such a surrender was what I wanted now above all else, even if it meant risking my very life to attain it.

Quickly I whispered my question to the clerk and was told that the girl was Miss Cynthia Louise Mische, daughter of *patrón* Louis Henry Mische of Bosque Redondo. The clerk suggested that she was a great beauty. I agreed that she was so indeed.

An open and honest approach to life has always been my preference, and so I now adjusted my collar wings and tugged my suit coat down on my shoulders. I marched directly forward to present myself to the *patrón* and to beg him to accept my introduction of myself to his daughter.

I was in something of a whirl and no doubt came across as being shyly awkward but indeed sincere. I myself have little recollection of exactly what words I spoke to the man, who by this time had advanced with his family nearly to the ballroom entrance, but the name I gave him was one that came easily and unbidden into my throat.

"Duncan Reeves, you said?" he repeated, eyeing me with as much amusement as interest. "All right, Mr. Reeves. A young man shouldn't have to celebrate alone in a strange city. Join us for the evening as our guest. And if you believe you can impress my Cindy more than the wild and woolly buckaroos she finds at home, why, make your best try, sir." He smiled and again I got the impression he was laughing beneath the surface. "I'm sure my wife at least would welcome the influence of a civilized gentleman at our table."

"Thank you, sir," I said in my nicest manner. "I am in your debt."

I most happily accepted my place between the ladies and without qualms ignored the obvious disdain of young Henry Mische. The evening and the opportunity could not have been more perfect.

# CHAPTER 26

This was a matter of grave importance, much more so than my work, and I could not possibly let them know that I was in truth the Jason Evers of whom they undoubtedly had heard much. At that time there were many ugly—and wholly untrue—stories circulating about me. These rumors arose due to the secret nature of my work for the railroad and could not have been denied by me without violation of the pledge of secrecy I had given Jamison when he hired me. I yet remain honor-bound to that pledge, but as some of those rumors still persist I will state here and now that never once during that period did I fire upon any man without just cause. This I do most firmly attest.

Still, I did not want it known by Cynthia Louise Mische that her new suitor was in fact the legendary, if much maligned, Jason Evers. I told her family that I had recently been engaged in business in Kansas City and was now seeking new opportunities in New Mexico Territory. This they accepted readily. It would have been obvious from my dress and choice of hotel that I was a gentleman and not impoverished.

I daresay that that evening I completely captivated Mrs. Mische and seemed to make some inroads with the object of my attentions as well. I was privileged to escort her to the dance floor for three separate sets, and even Louis Mische seemed to accept me into the group before the evening was done.

When we parted in the small hours of the morning Louis Mische—I believe at the suggestion of his wife—invited me to visit their home as a houseguest at the earliest opportunity.

I did not hesitate to accept, saying that business would delay me briefly in Santa Fe but that I would be only a few days behind them in reaching the Bar LM headquarters. Mische gave me detailed directions on how to reach the family home.

Immediately upon arising the next morning I wired Jamison to say that I would be unavailable for new assignments until further notice. I also wired my bank in Abilene to transfer my savings to a financial institution in Santa Fe. As this money was deposited in the name of Jason Evers I felt it best to make no personal appearance at the Santa Fe bank, but to make do with the amount I had on hand, which I judged to be adequate for the moment.

I also sold my pack mule and put my camp kit in storage at La Fonda. I thought it unlikely that a young gentleman newly arrived from Kansas City would be so completely equipped for lonely travel in the open country.

My good Winchester rifle I also put into storage, but I could not bring myself to leave the dependable .44 behind. After much thoughtful debate on the subject I packed it away in my saddle pockets, much as it had been when it first came into my possession.

I traded my old buckskin gelding also, as Jason Evers had been using that horse for a considerable length of time now, saddled the light-bodied bay mare I acquired in his place and rode eagerly south toward Bosque Redondo.

The Bar LM was smaller than I had anticipated and was much weathered. The main house was low and sprawling, made of thick mud walls covered with cracked and falling plaster and capped with heavy roof beams. The outbuildings were mostly large dugouts set into the flinty, dry soil of the hillsides. From the name of the area I had expected to find dense forests here, but instead was greeted by cedar and saltbrush and sparse grasses. Forested slopes could be seen on the mountains in the distance, while the country was even drier to the east toward the unseen Pecos. An unnamed stream ran through the headquarters toward the river.

"We've been on this land since the Fifties," Mische said proudly as he showed me around the place. "When we came here the Comanche were still coming this far down off the caprock and there was practically nothing to entertain the Apache between us and them either. We built sturdy to withstand raiders and fire arrows, but we've never seen the first red man on any piece of ground we use. Not counting the Pueblos, of course, and they don't bother anyone. At this point I don't expect we ever will. So I don't think you need to be frightened of anything here, Duncan."

"It could be that I don't frighten as easily as you expect, Mr. Mische," I told him.

"That's the spirit," he said warmly. He clamped a friendly hand onto my shoulder and squeezed hard enough that I thought he might leave bruises. I did not flinch.

"Don't let Pa's talk make you feel too easy," Henry warned. "This is still rough country out here. It ain't built up and civilized like in the city, and a man can still disappear and never be seen or heard from again if he gets into the wrong places or comes up onto the wrong people."

I thanked him politely, even though both of us knew he was not just being polite and thoughtful in his warning. Henry Mische had taken a dislike to me and was not much good at keeping that fact a secret.

I did have a champion inside the house, though, and that was equally obvious. Mrs. Mische thought it just fine that a young gentleman of quality would be interested in her daughter, particularly one not associated with this harsh and rather barren country so far removed from what she considered to be "real" civilization. She was very quick to tell me that Cynthia Louise's heritage was one of quality.

The Mische homeland had been the plantations and bayous of Louisiana, she said, the family removing to eastern Texas before her husband's birth. When it came time for him to take a wife it was only proper for him to return to Louisiana where her family, de Shong by name, was already connected to the Misches through several marital ties.

Both Henry and Cynthia Louise had been born in the soft, green country of east Texas, before Louis Mische resolved to move west in search of open land for his growing cattle operation. It was obvious that, even after so many years, Mrs. Mische still missed the greenery of Louisiana. She spoke often of New Orleans and of her family's annual excursions to that city when she was a girl.

As for Cynthia Louise herself, I saw little of her those first few days I was a guest in her home.

She was present at mealtimes but said little, her mother monopolizing the conversation on those occasions. During the daylight hours I was required to dutifully accompany her father and brother as they showed me over the grazing lands they ranged and proudly displayed to me a form of livestock at least as scrawny and bony and tick-infested as the animals I had known at home in Texas during my youth.

Only at night, when the family gathered around a small harpsichord in the main room of the house, did I see much of Cynthia. And even then she had little time for conversation, so intent was her mother on showing off Cynthia's talents at the keyboard, or as a hymnal soloist with her mother accompanying or as a reader of poetic works.

At least in that area I was able to participate, as while I had no musical talents whatsoever, the habit of reading instilled into me by Jonathon Keene so long before had remained with me ever since. Mrs. Mische's already high opinion seemed to increase after that ability was demonstrated in the recitals, and I showed my appreciation by presenting my hostess with a small volume of Burns that I had happened to be carrying in my saddle pockets.

On the morning of the fourth day I became bold enough (and in truth weary enough of the other) to beg off from the usual trip with the male Misches and ask Cynthia if I might use the family buggy and drive her out for a picnic in the open country. I was delighted by her shy acceptance of my invitation.

# CHAPTER 27

Although the girl had said next to nothing to me since my arrival at her home, she must have been taking a positive view of me during that time. The preparations for our picnic were extensive, so much so that it was nearing ten o'clock in the morning before we finally rolled out of the ranch yard with two large hampers tied behind the seat of the little covered rig. I was not at all unhappy at the choice of vehicles, made by whom I did not know, as the lone seat was so small that Cynthia was in close contact with me.

We drove upstream from the house to a cottonwood grove several miles westward of the headquarters. The spot was a cool and gentle oasis amid the dry and stony surroundings, and I wondered if Cynthia might have been brought here on family outings as a child.

"Will you help me prepare the picnic, Mr. Reeves?" she asked when I had tied the fancy light harness horse to a convenient limb.

"Of course."

One hamper held no food at all, but a light oilcloth to use as a ground cover, a tablecloth to put over it (very handsome cloth, but obviously too worn for table use now), fine linen napkins enough for half a dozen people and a selection of small pillows for our comfort. All of these Cynthia arranged to her satisfaction near the stream. I could not help but be pleased to see that the two mounds of pillows were placed side by side and not on opposite ends of the cloth.

"Do you want to set the food out now?" she asked.

"If you like." I carried the second and much heavier basket to its place on the cloth.

"I think it's *much* too early yet to eat, don't you, Mr. Reeves?"

"Yes, really."

She seemed quite shy now. She lowered herself onto a pillowed seat and sat with her hands in her lap, slim delicate fingers laced together, eyes cast primly down.

Lord, Lord, but she was lovely. Small and dainty and so very, very beautiful. Smooth, soft complexion. Long lashes lying dark against the swell of her cheeks. A tiny, rounded rosebud of a mouth. Long nose perhaps a touch out of proportion with the rest of her features, but refined and elegant nonetheless. Ears small and set close against her head. Neck slim and long and refined. I could see the flutter of pulse in the hollow of her throat, and I wanted to feel that flutter against my lips. I sat beside her.

She looked at me and I began to wonder if she knew how very painfully I was aware of the proud swell of her breasts beneath her blouse. I felt a surge of heat into my cheeks and was sure I must be blushing. Until that moment I had had little traffic with decent women, and the things I had learned with the other kind would not serve me here.

"Mr. Reeves."

"Yes?"

"May I ask you a very blunt question?"

"You may ask me anything you wish, Miss Mische." Her tone and my response were most properly formal.

"What are your intentions toward me, Mr. Reeves?"

It would be fair to say that I was shocked. It is certain that I was unprepared for such a question so very soon after meeting her. I must admit that my answer was more stammered than spoken. "I assure you. They are honorable. I hold you in . . . the highest regard. The very highest."

She nodded, and I thought that she was smiling. The

glimpse of her expression was too fleeting for me to be sure, for she again lowered her eyes and turned her head away.

She remained like that for some little time, and I began to wonder if I had offended her. When finally she turned back toward me, but still without looking directly at me, she said, "I thought they would be, Mr. Reeves. And no doubt I have shocked you by being so direct. You're from the East, after all, and could not be used to our western ways. This is a harder country out here, Mr. Reeves, and we often forget the niceties of Eastern customs. I really didn't mean to upset you. I did want to know. And the quickest way for me to find out was to ask."

"I just hope I . . . didn't offend you . . . by being so blunt . . ."

"No," she said quickly. "You don't offend me at all." She smiled shyly. "Mama and I have already discussed you, you know." She tossed her head coltishly and looked me in the eye.

"I didn't know."

She laughed, and it was a bright, musical sound. "You look so confused, Mr. Reeves. Please don't be." She reached forward and touched the tips of her fingers to my wrist. It was not at all reasonable, but I seemed to feel a great amount of heat in that small touch.

"What I wanted to do," she went on, "was to put you at ease, not chase you away." She laughed again and withdrew her hand. "I can promise you, you would have been most flattered if you had heard our conversations. You present a most favorable appearance."

I ducked my head, feeling quite foolish, and muttered a weak "thank you."

"It isn't all cut and dried, of course. Daddy will want to talk to you about your prospects."

"I really haven't any. Not at the moment."

Again she laughed. "You will have, then. Daddy and Henry can teach you all you need to know. Henry might be a bit impatient at times. He has this thing about being a *man*. But he's really very fair. Just a little protective sometimes. And he doesn't understand Eastern ways any more than you could understand ours yet. You will, though. They'll teach you all about it."

I was still confused. "What is it you're saying, Miss Mische?"

She giggled. "Silly goose. No, I shouldn't say that. Not even in fun. That's a perfect example right there. What I've just been telling you in a ladylike Western way is that my answer is yes. I will marry you. So from now on please call me Cynthia. Or Cindy if you'd rather. And I think it would be very nice if you would kiss me now, Duncan."

I was still quite reeling and senseless. I had come here infatuated with a beautiful but obviously unattainable young lady, and now we were betrothed. That was beyond anything I had truly expected, but now it was a fact.

I am afraid our first kiss was quite awkward in my state of numb confoundment, but we soon got over that and I found that a lady in one's arms was no more shy and a much greater delight to kiss than any common woman.

Before the picnic ended I even heard myself telling Cindy that I loved her. And it was true.

# CHAPTER 28

Back at the house, Mother Mische's response—it was very quickly established that that was what I was to call her—was one of unreserved approval. And if she thought we might have taken overlong on our picnic she never said a disapproving word within my hearing.

By the time the men of the house returned the engagement was an accomplished fact, but I think it surprised them as much as it had me. The women were already in private consultation about a suitable dress and other arrangements, so it was left to me to tell them.

The old man nodded and looked stern, but not exactly displeased at the prospect. Henry made no direct response and his face was a blank—deliberately, so I thought.

"Come into my study and we'll talk this over, Duncan," Louis said. "I think you should join us," he added when Henry started to fade back toward the kitchen.

I had not been in the study before and it was plain to see now that this was male territory only. The rest of the house was decorated with an eye for elegance and luxury. This small room was dark, with much wood and weapons and trophies of the hunt. Some of them were not from meat hunting either, as I recognized on the wall a crude bow and a clutch of arrows over which hung some dark scraps that I was almost certain were scalplocks. I asked about them.

"They are," he confirmed. "Kiowa. Used to be quite a problem in parts of Texas. That right there is why they aren't troublesome now."

"We aren't making you sick with that kind of talk, are we, Duncan?" Henry asked.

"No, you'd have to do a lot better than that," I returned with a smile. I did not get one back.

"Sit over there, Duncan, and put your feet up. Henry, you can pour us each a shot. After all, Duncan is fixing to become your brother, and that doesn't happen just every day."

The liquor was served and while I could not very easily refuse it under the circumstances I at least found it more palatable than the little I had tasted before.

"Now then, Duncan, tell me more about what it is you're planning for the future. For you and for my Cindy."

I repeated the story I had given him before about being on the scout for some new venture here in New Mexico.

As a matter of pure fact, I had not myself gotten far enough ahead in my thinking to give any time to worry about how I was going to support the two of us. It was already obvious that things were at an end for me with the railroad. I had a few dollars in the bank, but no idea what to use it on, and had no good asset like the old yellow horse again. I really did not know what I might do.

"You haven't talked to Cindy then about what she wants? Or expects?"

"No," I told him. "There hasn't been time for that yet. But of course I will do so at the first opportunity."

"Of course." He coughed once into his hand and glanced at his son. "I think I can pretty well tell you what she's going to say, Duncan. Cindy is what you might call the queen of the manor around here. She's looked up to. An' she likes that. She's said a good many times that she wants to go on living here. Travel to the cities from time to time, but make her home right here." Again he glanced over toward Henry, and this time I was wondering if it was worry or warning he was directing that way.

"We sat down with both Cindy an' Henry a long time ago, Duncan, an' we let the both of them know that us old

folks won't be around forever. Our home and holdings here,
our livestock, whatever we got in the bank, half of it be-
longs to each of them, Henry an' Cindy alike. You follow?"

"It sounds pretty simple, but you're a long way from
dead. Maybe you better tell me."

"All right, boy, what I'm saying is this. When you marry
Cindy you're taking on a responsibility for half of this place
besides. I run it for now, an' when I'm gone Henry will run
it. But you are responsible for Cindy's half of it." He tossed
the last of his drink down. "Duncan, we, all of us, are gonna
expect you to hold up your end of the work."

"If you can."

"*Henry!*" the old man barked. "That wasn't called for."

"Maybe he had a point anyway," I told them. "I've never
pretended to know anything about cows or ranching."

Louis Mische smiled. "Hell, boy, I know that. You'd never
have gotten Cynthia or her momma, bless her soul, interested in you if you had. They wanted bigger game than
some cowhand." He chuckled. "The truth is I always expected that girl to hook herself some English gentleman.
Well, I'm just as glad she didn't. The ones that end up here
seem to be a pretty poor lot if you ask me. I figure she's
done better by finding a good, honest American, even if you
do have a lot to learn. You seem bright enough. I don't think
you'll have any trouble learning what you need to know."

I suppose that was intended as a compliment, but it
seemed a bit left-handed. Still, the whole thing was a stroke
of fortune. And if Cindy liked the nicer things in life I saw
no reason why she shouldn't have them, here and in New
York and Chicago and all the grand places I had heard of.
It did sound like we would be able to afford that and more.

"From now on, Duncan," Mische went on, "I want you
and Henry to work close together. I want you an' him to get
up together every morning and stay together right through
to supper.

"Henry, you're to show this young gentleman just what it

means to be a cowman, you hear? Whatever you do during
the day, you tell him what it is you're doing an' why it has
to be done. Right? And don't just tell him neither. A man
can't learn much just from looking and listening. You let
him get in there an' *do* after he's seen something a time or
two. You understand me, son?"

"Yessir."

"You, Duncan?"

"I, uh, I guess I do."

"Are you having second thoughts about this?"

"No, not that."

"What, then?"

I gave him one of my best smiles. "I was thinking that I
might look a bit silly chasing cattle while I'm wearing a
good suit and cravat. If you wouldn't mind, maybe I could
ride to town before we start this learning program of yours."

"Stockton isn't too awful far. Henry can take you over
there tomorrow."

"I'd prefer to go up to Santa Fe," I said.

The old man's eyebrows went up a notch.

I grinned at him. "There's more likely to be a decent jew-
eler's there, sir. Miss Cynthia certainly deserves a proper engagement ring."

Well now, that part did it. And when it was repeated to
Mrs. Mische it went over even bigger. She was in a regular
flutter about it and went dashing off to tell Cynthia what a
fine and thoughtful gentleman she was to have as her husband. And to prepare a list of materials I should bring back
for the making of the gown. By the time they were done,
and it was plenty late that night, the list was large enough
that I had to drive the family gig rather than burden a saddle horse with so much load.

I made it to the city all right, still feeling in something of
a whirl myself, and spent a few days doing my shopping,
charging the Mische purchases to their accounts as instructed.

For myself I got some rough work clothing and a durable pair of heavy boots so I would not unduly abuse my good glove-leather ones. I also picked up cheap a fancy-looking ring that the fellow assured me was set with real diamonds. Since they did not break when I rapped on them I believed him.

The most important thing—and the reason I had had to come to the city, alone, instead of riding down to Fort Stockton with Henry looking over my shoulder—was one I put off until last. I guess in a way I had been avoiding it. Once I did it my bridges were burned and there was no turning back. I went to the telegraph office and wired Jamison: TERMINATING AGREEMENT THIS DATE STOP NO FORWARDING ADDRESS.

I will admit that I was feeling a little shaky when I went back outside and climbed into the Mische rig to begin the long drive south. The railroad had been straight with me and always had come to my defense when I needed them. I felt alone again now for the first time in a long while.

# CHAPTER 29

Henry Mische and I really were not on the very best of terms anyway, and it did nothing for the relationship when he came into my room at five o'clock A.M. and dragged me out of my bed. Until that time I had at least been able to sleep until seven or so. Now it turned out that, until then, they had been serving breakfast on company-in-the-house hours, and Louis and Henry had been getting up before me and getting some work done before breakfast, too. I would not have been insulted if they had kept that up.

Then Henry compounded the annoyance by scoffing at my comfortable old Army saddle.

"We ain't going for a canter in the park today, Dunk," he said. This was his first use of a nickname I came to despise. "Here." He picked up and threw at me a dirt-crusted, ugly old lump of a saddle that weighed three times what mine did and was perhaps half as comfortable. "You can use this one 'til you get one of your own made. It don't look like much, but I learned to rope out of it. I guess you can too."

"I'm not a roper," I told him.

"You will be."

I had my doubts, but let that pass.

They fitted me out with *chaparejos* to protect my legs and leather gloves with heavy gauntlets to protect my hands and a leather vest to protect my chest, and I began to wonder if we were going to be looking after cattle or riding out to a jousting tourney against neighboring knights or dragons or such.

Henry selected a horse for me and roped it out of the

using band confined in a little trap near the house. I was more than half expecting him to put me up on a particularly wild one and was hoping that he would. I might not be skilled in the ways of a cowhand, but I could by God ride and I was willing to prove it. There was no opportunity for that, though, as the horse he chose was neither ranker nor milder than any of the others, and once caught and fairly settled was set for a day's business.

Henry and the old man and I rode out from the headquarters together. In a draw a few miles from the house we met two Mexican vaqueros.

"This is Enrique, Duncan," the old man said, "and that gray-headed old coyote there is Salvatore. They live over the hill there a little way and help us work this place."

Both of them nodded and grinned and looked me over. I got the impression they already knew who I was. I wondered just what all they might have heard in that regard. Whatever it had been, though, they did not seem hostile.

It turned out that Enrique was old Sal's second oldest son. They had lived here since long before the Misches came and sort of went with the place. When the men weren't working with Louis Mische they worked around home, where they raised some hand-irrigated scratch corn and the kids watched over some long-haired goats. I never visited there, but saw the place from a distance a number of times.

Louis talked to them awhile in Spanish and Henry told me they were telling him they had seen some beeves drifting toward a particularly boggy place that ought to be checked soon. We split up then, the old man riding with the Mexicans and Henry taking me in tow.

When they were gone Henry turned to me and gave me a cold look. "You don't *look* like your nose is out of joint, Dunk. Are you feeling put out because Poppa rode off with those Mexicans instead of us?"

"Of course not," I said. "Somebody has to keep an eye on

them, or they'll be drawing wages from him and sleeping under a tree the day long. I can understand that."

Henry made a sour face and spat down past his boot toe. "You're an Easterner all right." He stood in his stirrups to stretch his legs for a moment and rolled himself a cigarette. He flipped his spent match away and said, "Listen, Dunk. Rico and Sal are good people. They *belong* here, you know? They get fifty cents a day's work for the two of them an' they're worth four times that. They know as much what needs doing here as we do an' they'd do everything they ought to, and more, if we didn't see them but once a year an' forgot to pay them when we did. And they wouldn't overcharge us a nickel's worth even then. What I'm saying is that they're *straight*." He shook his head angrily and resettled his hat.

"The thing is, Dunk, Poppa has this idea that you an' me oughta be put together, just the two of us alone, so we can learn to work together in the same set of harness. He figures we're gonna be side by side for a long time to come. An' I guess that's true enough *if* you marry Cindy. Well, there ain't none of this my idea, Dunk, but I'll do whatever Poppa says an' so will you. Right?"

I shrugged. It had been a long, *long* time since anyone told me what to do.

"Yeah, well, you got a right to know that there ain't none of this is my idea, but I'm going to make the best of it. I'll show you what I can an' when I'm done Poppa will take over, and between us we'll make a cowman of you so you won't end up shaming Cindy with your ignorance. And while I'm on the subject I'll tell you here an' now, Dunk, if you ever shame her in any other way I will personally stomp you right down into the ground, boy."

Young Henry had his jaw stuck out and his eyes just positively afire with righteous passion when he said that, and perhaps he expected me to cower before his zeal. He would, of course, have spoken quite differently to Jason Evers than he did to Duncan Reeves, the difference in Henry's physical size and mine notwithstanding.

I looked him straight in the eye so as to show him I would take none of his water and I said, "If that day ever comes, Henry, you will receive a great surprise. Now why don't you stop wasting your father's time and mine and start showing me what to do with these damn cows."

Henry grunted and ground out the butt of his cigarette on his saddle horn and spurred his horse into a gallop. I had to go some to catch him.

It turned out that Henry and I were the ones assigned to check the bog, but we had work to do before we ever got there.

It seemed that working range cattle meant that man and horse had to forsake the natural order of things and always choose the most difficult path from one place to the next.

Instead of finding the open and easy routes where we rode, Henry rode into and through the densest and the thorniest patches of brush he could find. And for so barren a country it was truly amazing how much brush-choked scrub a man could find.

"These old ladinos are nine parts wild to one part tame," Henry said over his shoulder. "They'll lay up in the thorn to hide an' the worst of them only come out to eat at night. You got to shove them outside or they'll spend a lifetime an' never be touched."

So we rode through the thorn patches that any sensible man would circle around and when there were none in our path we detoured from side to side to find some. I began to be glad for the hot, heavy leather armor we wore.

"D'you notice the brands on those steers?" he asked at one point.

"What steers?"

Henry turned in his saddle to point a raised eyebrow my way. "Jesus Christ, Dunk, I'm tryin' to get you to notice brands and you ain't even seen the steers. Three of 'em. Moving out of our way over to the right there."

"I've been following you. How the hell was I supposed to know you wanted me to look for cows too?"

"Well *look* for 'em, dammit."

I gave him back stare for stare and had the satisfaction of seeing a mesquite limb rake across his chest and shoulders before he turned back to watch where he was going. If it hurt he did not show it.

A little while later I did see a brown back disappearing into the brush on our left.

"I saw that one," I called to him.

"A steer?"

"Uh-huh."

"The hell. That was a cow. Didn't you see the calf at her side? Steers don't have calves, Dunk. Try an' remember that."

It was difficult to do, but I restrained myself and kept quiet. It seemed that my future brother-in-law was a sarcastic sonuvabitch.

When we reached the bog, which looked like it was a pond for some part of the year and a nuisance the rest of the time, there was indeed an ignorant bovine trapped in the soft mud. A mud-daubed calf was on firmer ground nearby and was noisily announcing its mother's predicament.

"She's gotta come out or they'll both die," Henry said. "Can you throw a rope, Dunk?"

"You know I can't."

"Then I'll work from the saddle an' you on the ground."

Which sounded all right to me until I learned what was involved.

Henry took up his rope and shook out a loop with a deftness I knew I would neither have nor really want in the future. He gave it a twirl and the loop floated out to wrap neatly around the cow's horns. The animal blinked and jerked her head when the hemp slapped her across the eyes.

"You want a horn catch for this," Henry said. "Not down on the throat."

The other end of the rope was tied to his saddle horn. He swung his horse's rump and urged the gelding ahead, but the light cow pony could not begin to pull the cow free of the sucking mud. I was a little surprised that the cow's neck did not break before Henry accepted this.

"Your turn," he said finally. I thought he said it with some pleasure.

My job, it transpired, was to wade into the muck alongside the cow and dig the clinging goo away from her legs. It was a sweaty, filthy, miserable job that took me more than an hour to complete. And all the while Henry sat there on his horse, keeping a slight strain on the rope and smoking his cigarettes and smiling.

When finally the stupid beast was free and on solid ground, having transferred the mud from herself onto my person in the process, Henry grinned and said, "Best get on your horse before I turn loose of her. She'll be mad now." His grin got wider. "An' kinda watch her too. She'll be thirsty as hell by now. Often as not the fool things run back into the same damn bog an' you gotta do it over again."

Even my desire to prevent that from happening was not enough to lend strength or speed to my legs as I dragged myself back into my saddle. For the first time that day I was glad it was a borrowed saddle and not my own, for I must have been carrying twenty pounds of sticky, drying goo on each leg of my chaps.

It was no wonder, I thought, that cowhands smelled bad and were mostly crazy. They were entitled to it.

# CHAPTER 30

The evenings were not so long nor so convivial now as they had been when I was company. As family, or close to being family, I came in as worn down as Louis and Henry and there was no more sitting up late into the night singing and listening to Cynthia play the harpsichord.

One advantage to the new status, though, was that it was understood that Cynthia and I should be allowed our privacy after dinner. I was generally too tired to want to drive anywhere, but we would walk out into the darkness for a few minutes of whispering and hugging or would sit in the bench swing on the covered porch at the front of the ugly, sprawling, mud-walled house.

"Someday," Cynthia told me, "I hope you will build us a house of our own. A fine one, made of lumber, two stories tall and with polished floors and brocade draperies at the windows."

I promised her that I would, and knew that she would be content for a long time to come with the planning of her house.

While she was doing that Mother Mische was busy planning for the wedding. She seemed in something of a quandary over the setting of the date. Too soon would not be seemly, but neither did she want to delay it. After much mealtime consultation we set it for the third Saturday in August, for reasons which the women may have understood but I never did.

Louis I saw at meals and as we left each morning for the

day's work. The bulk of my time, though, was spent in Henry's company.

He tried for hours to teach me the tricks of fine roping. To him it was an art as important as any and more than most and was something he did for its own sake and not merely for practicality.

He showed me over and over again, but in truth I did not and do not care how to throw a loop in a figure eight so as to catch the hind feet separately in each end of the 8 or, vertically, to catch the head in one end and the forelegs in another, or any of the other fancy catches that pleased him so.

Still, I have always been quick with my hands and a ready learner, and I was able to learn the simple head catch, which, once shown, is not greatly more difficult than learning to throw a rock with accuracy. Beyond that minimum working tool I did not care to learn.

I learned to do that and to throw an animal and keep it from rising, to castrate a bull calf and to clean out the rice-grain-looking larvae of screwworms and to doctor their wounds with a coating of turpentine and fish oil and peppers, bottles of which smelly stuff were always available in our saddle pockets.

I did *not* learn to accept the smell of manure and sweat and dirt that clung to me at the end of each day, and I was always eager to wash before dining, which the men seemed not to understand, even though the women of the family approved.

Henry seemed quite totally disgusted with me as a working partner until the day we rode past a sleeping rattler and, before Henry could take down his rope to whip it to death, I shot its head off with the little .32 I still carried in my pocket.

"Damn, that was good shooting, Dunk. And fast. Where'd an Eastern fella learn to shoot like that?"

"There was a cutbank behind my home back in KC," I told him. "I used to spend a lot of time practicing."

"Well, I reckon. But hell, Dunk, you oughta carry a man's gun instead of that little thing. You just don't seem to understand such things, but out here it's all right for a man to wear a gun. Everybody does it."

I suppose that should have struck me as funny, but it did not. I was long since overtired of Henry's condescending ways about my supposed Eastern background.

"If you want I'll loan you a proper revolver, Dunk."

"I have one back in my room," I told him.

Henry gave me a look that had more than a trace of contempt in it. "You can use it, all right. Why don't you carry it?" He left the question hanging there as if unfinished, and I knew the rest of it would have been was I afraid to wear a gun where other men carried theirs.

"I don't have a holster for it."

"I have an old one you can use."

"All right," I said. "Drag it out tonight." I had never used a holster for my .44 and did not especially want to now, but I could not possibly carry the gun in my usual way here. That habit was too well known as belonging to Jason Evers. And while the Mische family knew me as Duncan Reeves, their friends who came to celebrate the wedding would be meeting a stranger. I wanted to arouse no suspicions.

"We'll see how well you can shoot, Dunk."

"Yeah."

That night he gave me the holster and I stayed awake an extra half hour getting used to it in the privacy of my room. Letting the thing flop on my hip was nearly as slow as getting to the .32 in my pocket, but I found that by pulling it around in front of my belly I could get the big Colt out nearly as quickly as usual.

The next morning Henry grinned when he saw me wearing it.

"Say, Dunk, that isn't the way you wear a gun. Here . . ."

He started to reach for it, I suppose to move it into what he considered a proper position.

I really didn't mean to do it. I certainly didn't take time to think about it and come to a conscious decision. But I guess in the past few years I had gotten a little touchy about the idea of anyone taking my gun from me.

Before Henry's hand could reach my waist I had the .44 out and the muzzle was tucked up near his nose. He almost went cross-eyed looking into the bore and he became more than a little pale.

Me, I felt myself go hot around the ears and knew I would be getting red in the face. I shoved the gun back into the holster.

Henry backed up a step and tried to smile, but it didn't come off too well.

"Sorry," I told him. "I, uh, didn't mean to scare you."

"Is that thing loaded?"

"I'm . . . not sure." It was, of course, and I knew it was, but I thought it an appropriate time to be stupidly Eastern. "I'll check if you like . . . Yeah, I guess it is. Sorry."

"I thought you didn't . . ." He let the sentence die.

"I told you. I practiced a lot back home. You know. Broken bottles. Clods of dirt. Like that."

"Sure. Like that." He still looked shaken, but he managed a weak smile. "I was gonna spend some time today showing you how to draw and fire."

I managed to keep from laughing and with a straight face told him, "I'll be glad to get some pointers from you, Henry."

"I don't think so, Duncan. No, I really don't think so." Henry turned and hurried away toward the kitchen, where breakfast would be waiting. I took a little time to readjust the buckles on my chaps before I followed.

# CHAPTER 31

Guests began arriving for the wedding several days in advance, some of them coming from Santa Fe and more from the sparsely populated sections of New Mexico and west Texas and even over into Arizona. There was even one rockaway loaded with distant-cousin Misches who had made the long haul from east Texas just for the event. Mother Mische complained frequently that there was no one left to represent the Louisiana de Shongs, her last known relative having gone to the mining camps of Colorado some years before.

The house became the exclusive province of the women, while the men were obliged to bunk in the outbuildings or wagons or wherever they could find room for a blanket.

Rico and old Sal helped set up long trestle tables in the yard where everyone could eat, which seemed to be a day and night preoccupation with most of the guests. Once the tables were in place the two Mexicans disappeared. Any ranch work that would be done for the next few days, they would have to do.

No one had thought to hire a band, but none was needed. There were enough musical instruments in the guests' wagons to fit out several town bands, and there were twice that number of musicians to play them when the owner tired or decided to take a fling at the dancing.

There was little in the way of rowdiness or drinking, but there was no end to the joke-telling and ribald suggestions, myself the butt of most of them. I did my best to keep smiling throughout.

The preacher, a man named LeRoi O'Donnell, arrived with the first of the guests and was as interested in jug-nipping and dancing as anyone.

Cynthia I saw little of during those hectic few days, she being mostly confined to the house, from which I was excluded.

The afternoon before the ceremony was to take place a handsome, bright-polished rig rolled into the yard, pulled by a matched pair of bays with plumes in their manes and with coats as shiny as the carriage wood. The men seemed to recognize the driver and set up a loud hullo. Indeed, the old gentleman looked familiar to me also, and from his dignified dress I began to wonder if the governor had chosen to attend my wedding. I was distracted, though, by a well-wisher, and by the time I turned again to look he and his lady had disappeared among the guests.

That evening, the night before the wedding, a special dinner was planned. There was no possible way to accommodate everyone with chairs, but the bride and groom and family were to have special treatment for this meal.

Someone—no doubt quite a few someones—managed to carry the huge old dining table outdoors, and an elegant service for five was laid on the linen, Cynthia and myself being placed at the center where we would face the guests.

While that was going on I and Louis and Henry were being urged into our best clothing, which had mysteriously appeared in the root cellar, the suits freshly brushed, shirts washed and collars boiled rigid in potato water.

As soon as the sun disappeared and the cool of the evening set in we were escorted to the table, where Cynthia and her mother joined us.

Cynthia . . . ah, what can I say? She was even more lovely now than on the first evening I saw her. She wore the same ribbon and cameo brooch as she had that night, but a new gown of the palest yellow, just enough color in it to set off the green of her eyes, and an emerald-green sash. Her hair was perfectly coiled and pinned to show off the delicacy of her throat and features, and she carried a bouquet of the bright yellow, wild-growing brown-eyed Susans that are so much prettier than their name.

I bowed over her hand and seated her at the table and we received a round of cheers from our guests. That freely given outpouring of affection and goodwill pleased and touched me perhaps even more than any degree of respect Jason Evers ever earned. This I say in all candor.

Dinner for all this crowd consisted of a whole steer roasted slowly over mesquite coals, and another had been slaughtered and spitted and was already cooking in anticipation of the post-wedding ceremony. I am certain the meal was an excellent one, but this I could not judge for myself. Cynthia and I were so busy accepting congratulations and good wishes from our guests that we rarely had time to place fork to mouth and certainly had no chance to savor what little we were able to eat.

Perhaps by custom—and this I would not know—the tradition of wedding gifts here was fulfilled by our cattleman guests in the form of giving to us a heifer calf from each of them as the seed stock of a herd to be branded in our own style (I had no brand of my own, of course) and run on the Bar LM land with the others of the family herds. A few other guests of city backgrounds deposited on the table fine lamps or serving pieces which brought bright joy to my beloved's eyes, and I was reminded anew that I had found a lady of great quality who would appreciate the elegant things I intended to give her.

It was a glorious evening, and when the dining and gifting were done I led Cynthia in the first dance of the night. She floated before me as delicate as mist and I was truly happy.

Later, when Cynthia had been spirited back into the house where she would remain unseen until the morrow's ceremony, I circulated among our guests and enjoyed their company and their merriment.

Under one of the hanging lanterns I found my soon-to-be brother-in-law in conversation with the finely dressed gentleman who had arrived that afternoon. Still curious, I joined them.

"We were just talking about you, Dunk," Henry said as I came near. Neither of us had made any attempt to be close to the other since the morning I had frightened him so badly, but even so he sounded unusually cold. I regretted that and, in the warmth of my humor, resolved to try to make him my friend and brother in the future and to tell him so at the first opportunity.

That chance was not now, though, for he mumbled an introduction and hurried away into the night.

"I'm sorry, sir. I didn't catch your name," I told the gentleman who was still standing beside me.

"Charles Goode, Mr. Reeves." We shook hands, and he gave me a long look.

"You've been a very lucky young man, Duncan."

"Yes, I have, sir. Cynthia is a fine girl, and her family is as fine as she. I am indeed luckier than most. And thank you." It seemed a perfectly normal congratulation from a guest.

"How did that yellow horse work out for you?"

"Sir?" I genuinely had no idea what he was talking about.

"The yellow horse I sold you some years back, Duncan. Or perhaps you don't remember him. Very fast as I recall, but absolutely no good with cattle."

I was startled, taken completely by surprise, but not to the point of insensibility. And I have always been quick of mind. Charles Goode. Charlie. The wealthy old New Mexico rancher we had visited after leaving El Paso. He was groomed and dressed for visiting now and no longer was limping, but this was the same man. I remembered him now —it was no wonder he had looked familiar to me when he drove in.

But it was all right, I realized nearly as quickly. I had been going under the name Duncan Reeves at that time, too, and that would be the way he would remember me.

Some time soon I would have to mention to the Misches, casually, that I had once spent a summer traveling in the Southwest with a peddler. In fact, as soon as possible I should mention having met Charles Goode then and express my delight at seeing him again. But it would be all right. He did know me as Duncan Reeves.

All of this I understood without having to think it through, and before an awkward amount of time had passed I was able to smile and tell him how good it was to see him again.

"The horse worked out just fine, sir. I never worked cattle then, and he took me safely back to Missouri." Which certainly was no lie. I have always prided myself on my honesty. "But I haven't heard of Mr. Keene since that summer. How is he?" The question was a crucial one, and I was thinking rapidly and well enough to know it. Jon had told Goode nothing about me then, but if they had visited more recently there might have been more said. After all, Jon was the one who had first warned me how much men will talk. Much of what he had taught me was coming back to mind now.

"I wouldn't know," Goode said. "I haven't heard anything of Jon in years now."

"I'm sure we both hope he is well, then," I said.

Goode agreed and we talked for a few minutes more. About how fine a man Jon Keene was. About the prospects of the cattle market (of which I knew nothing, but had heard Louis and Henry speak) and other such trivialities.

After a little time Goode excused himself and went to greet another gray-haired rancher.

I turned and went in search of Henry. I wanted to tell him about my resolution to be friendlier with him in the future. And about learning that Charles Goode was a past acquaintance.

I could not find Henry that evening, however, and eventually had to conclude that he had found a willing filly among the visiting daughters and that he would be out of sight for a time.

It was late that night before I finally got to bed, and I was exhausted. Much too tired to deal with the nagging thought that there was something not quite right about something—I could not think what—that Charles Goode had said.

# CHAPTER 32

The morning was quite beautiful . . . and I was very nervous. The best thing that could be said about my feelings that day was that at least I did not have to suffer them for long. Thanks to the late hour of the previous night's merriment I had to be wakened just barely in time to prepare for my own wedding.

It was Louis who awakened me, already dressed and in something of a state of agitation.

"Well, at least *you* are here. For a while there I thought you'd disappeared too," he said.

"Too? Is Cynthia . . . ?"

"Cindy? Hell no. But I guess the whole damn houseful over there is going crazy. Trying to get her ready an' calm Mother too. Damn good thing I'm stuck out here with the men."

"Then who . . . ?" I had visions of the preacher being missing or something.

My soon-to-be father-in-law looked momentarily startled, then said, "Oh yeah. I didn't say. It's that damned Henry. Can't find him anywhere. An' every girl on the grounds seems to be accounted for, close as we can figure it anyhow." Louis shook his head wearily. "If that boy is sleeping off a drunk in a gully somewhere he's gonna find out he isn't too damn big for me to take my razor strop to, by God. Breaking his mama's heart, he is. An' you'd best get ready or you'll catch it too. Hop to it, Duncan."

"Yeah." I rubbed my eyes and wished I didn't have to shave this particular morning. I was not entirely certain my hand would be steady and did not want to stand up for my own wedding with a dewlap cut into my cheek.

"Move, boy."

"Yessir."

The ceremony was held outdoors and was proof positive that someone had been up awfully early or maybe had never gotten to bed. A pole arbor had been built in the yard where the big table had sat the night before, and someone had laced cedar branches into the poles so it was all shady and green. It was a pretty sight.

The preacher set up in the middle, of course, and I was on one side. It had been planned that Henry was to stand up beside me, but now he could not be found, so Louis dragged up one of his friends whose name I was too nervous to remember if I ever heard it.

One of the ladies set the harpsichord to tinkling—it was in the yard too—and here came Cynthia and her mama out from the house. Mother Mische transferred her to Louis's arm and they made a solemn march to the arbor.

Lord, but she took my breath away. She was wearing a gown of the purest white, made of some shiny material and covered all over with white lace. White sash. White lace veil. Carrying a long bouquet of bright red flowers that were no redder than her lips. I came near to swooning when I saw her.

I remember every step of her march toward me, and Louis placing her hand into mine, yet none of it seemed to take any time at all.

Of the ceremony itself I recall little. I remember the sound of the preacher's voice, but not his words. I remember speaking in response and hearing Cynthia do so as well. The next thing I remember clearly is Cynthia lifting the veil back from her face, and the shining clarity of the trust in her eyes. I kissed her softly, there in front of everyone, and we were man and wife.

The guests set up a cheering and surged forward around

us like spring floodwaters until I thought we would drown.
The musical-minded guests took over from the lady at the
harpsichord and stepped up the pace and we must have
been dancing for more than an hour before someone, probably Mother Mische, remembered the cake.

So we all formed up around a table bearing a sugar-
frosted white cake, and Cynthia and I cut the first piece and
shared it, and everyone cheered again.

We had dinner about the middle of the afternoon, not
getting time to enjoy this one any more than we had the
first one, and immediately afterward we were picked up and
removed.

A flock of giggling girls picked Cynthia up bodily and
carried her away. A bunch of horse-laughing younger men
and older boys grabbed me and mauled me into the house
and into the big room that had been Cynthia's and now
would be ours together.

She was already there waiting.

I was scarcely aware of the rest of the commotion as the
girls who had escorted her kissed her cheeks and one by one
went giggling from the room. It seemed a long time until
we were alone and I could shut and lock the door.

If she felt shy with me I would not wonder. I did myself.

"Are you afraid?"

She nodded.

I crossed the room and sat beside her on the broad bed. I
slipped an arm around her waist as I had done often enough
before, but this time she did not yield to me.

"It will be all right," I promised her. "We have time."

She smiled then and seemed to relax somewhat.

I took my coat and tie off and removed my collar. I
stretched out on the bed and after a time she loosened up
enough to lie beside me in my arms, and it was good to
have her there. I kissed her forehead and enjoyed the feel of
her breath against my neck.

We must both have been very tired, for we drifted into sleep like that, quiet and secure and very, very pleasant.

Someone was pounding on the door as if to break it down. It was very dark, only a crack of light showing under the door. For a moment it was hard to remember where I was, but soon I did. If this was someone's idea of a shivaree it was a poor one.

I disengaged myself from Cynthia and slipped off of the bed. Dimly I remembered seeing a lamp on the night table beside the bed and a metal box near it. I found the box by feel, and the matches it held.

Someone had moved my things into the room and by habit I pulled the old .44 Army from my saddlebags as I passed the dresser on my way to the door. I shoved the long barrel down into my waistband and turned the lock bolt.

Henry stood there in the lamplight, haggard and unshaven and dirty. He was still wearing the clothing I had last seen him in.

Behind him was his father. And behind them Charles Goode.

All three looked fiercely angry. Henry held a large caliber Remington revolver already in his hand.

Behind me I heard Cynthia stir in her sleep and the faint rustle of her beautiful wedding gown as she shifted position. I began to get angry myself.

"What the hell is this?" I looked each of them in the eyes, one by one, Henry and Louis and finally Goode.

Seeing Charles Goode there and his anger . . . it was like turning a key. Of a sudden I remembered what had been out of place when he spoke to me the night before.

He had said he sold me a yellow horse. Yet as far as he knew then he had swapped the yellow to Jonathon Keene. He had known nothing about me owning that bay horse he took in trade, nor that the yellow was to be mine.

If he knew the yellow was mine he had talked to Jon. He had talked to him *after* that fight down in Arizona when the freighter tried to cheat me. And Jon had known me all along as Jason Evers and not Duncan Reeves. And there was no one this side of the Mississippi who would not have heard of Jason Evers, especially the lies told of me during my railroad employment years, when to protect them I could not speak out to defend myself.

The Misches would have heard those lies too.

"Jason Evers," Henry said. His voice was ugly and his face twisted. "I've been to the telegraph for a description of you. The law is on its way. Leave my sister be and get out of this house, you sonuvabitch."

The muzzle of his pistol began to rise toward my belly.

The faithful .44 that had served me so well for so long came now into my hand again and the burn of the powder was so near that it set Henry's shirt afire.

I admit here in the deepest and truest honesty that of all I have done in this life, the killing of Henry Mische I most regret. Would to God that he had not thrown down on me that night, but he did and I had no choice save to defend my life and no weapon save such an ultimate one.

So he died and I was forced to flee from my wedding chamber while Louis Mische and Charles Goode were taking cover against shots I never directed toward them, and the last sight I had of my bride was her white and startled face in the lamplight while I raced past her toward the windows and a hastily borrowed horse.

# CHAPTER 33

That ugly day in August, 1871, was the last time I saw my dear wife. In the seven years intervening I have written to her often, but not since the first months have I felt free to provide her with a return address.

It is well known that Louis Mische placed a wholly illegal and improper bounty on my head, and in the first year following the incident I was twice obliged to kill strangers who had been sent against me with no more of the right on their side than the lure of Mische's dollars. Since that time interest in collecting the bounty seems to have waned.

From the Bosque Redondo I rode north into Colorado, passing by without caring to visit the site of the McComb battle, and sought the comforts and high living of the rich silver districts. There among the lofty peaks I have passed the years since my unfortunate separation from my wife, who would be at my side now but for her brother's untrusting impulsiveness and her father's desire for vengeance. This, too, I must regret.

I might state now also that it is true that I was a frequent companion of—and I believe a true and honest friend to—"Pine" Jack Kutts and Logan Wamball, but if either of those gentlemen was engaged in theft of mining properties or in any other impropriety at that time I was completely unaware of such activity.

Their deaths at the hands of Vigilance Committee members I still regard as unjustified, as I would gladly have testified had not the excitement of the moment caused the Committee to be unjustly suspicious of me also. I feel I need make no apologies for leaving that area without stopping to enter a defense argument, as I have learned that prudence often allows time for the passions to ebb and for cooler heads to prevail.

Nor is it true, as my detractors would claim, that I was ever employed as a hired "enforcer" by the so-called Cherry Creek Gang of wealthy Denver financiers and mine operators.

I will state freely and with affectionate pride that I was indeed acquainted with most if not all of the gentlemen so named by those who are envious of their undeniable business acumen, but neither I nor, to my knowledge, they at any time engaged in any activities that were illegal or might be considered improper.

I spent many enjoyable hours in their company contesting with cards and with billiard cues, but at no time was the subject of kill-for-pay employment ever raised. Had it been, our friendship would have been terminated immediately.

I earned my living during this period in a variety of ways, none of them either remarkable or exciting, mostly dealing here and there in stock certificates or mining shares. It is also true that the turn of the pasteboards has been quite good to me, and I am considered to be an accomplished card player.

My current circumstances—soon to be corrected—came about as the result of mischance of the most malicious kind.

At the request of a trusted friend, I entrained at Denver and rode south to the elegant community of Colorado Springs, intending to speak on my friend's behalf with Mr. Burton Dore, who held certain shares of interest to my friend. Written communication between them had not proven effective and it was hoped that a personal appeal might persuade Mr. Dore to part with the shares at a fair market price.

On arriving at the Springs—misnamed, I might add, as there are in fact no springs in Colorado Springs—I learned that Mr. Dore might be located in Manitou Springs nearby (where there is an actual mineral spring to justify its name), where he had reportedly gone on business. I engaged a rig and was driven there within the hour, the two communities being in close proximity.

I found Mr. Dore that afternoon and engaged him in a conversation in the privacy of a small office borrowed for that purpose. It is important to note that this conversation took place behind closed doors, with no one present except Mr. Dore and myself.

I presented my friend's offer and was most rudely rebuffed.

"You're a bunch of thieving sons of bitches," Dore exclaimed, "and you ruin people to fatten your own pockets. Well, not me, mister. Not this time. You can go find yourself another carcass to pick. You won't be able to steal the sweat of the boys who built the Lady M."

"Mr. Dore," I assured him, "I am only delivering a message for a friend. I know nothing about the Lady M or who built her. I do, sir, object to your choice of language and will not put up with it. I suggest you do not speak that way to Jason Evers, sir."

My mention of my name, well known as it is, was intended to calm him, not to goad him. However, it had an unfortunate effect.

Dore's face paled and his eyes went wide. "My God, you've come to kill me."

It was my intention to assure him that this was not the case, that I had come only as a favor. His fear, however, made this impossible, and his hand dropped into his pocket. When he produced a revolver I had no choice but to defend myself, which I did.

Dore fell with a bullet in his chest which incapacitated him, although he was not mortally wounded.

There was an almost immediate outcry at the closed door, and I thought it best to retire from the scene until emotions might cool. I was at the window when two men burst into the room with pistols drawn. One fired a shot that passed near my ear and shattered the glass of the window.

I snapped a shot at him, felling him instantly with a bullet that entered his eye socket.

I aimed again at the remaining man and attempted to cock my old .44 Colt Army, only to feel the hammer lie slack under my thumb. The mainspring of the old gun was broken.

Before I could reach the little .32 in my pocket the second man had leveled his pistol on me and others were pouring into the office, one of them with a shotgun in his hands. I had no choice but to give myself up into their custody.

The trial that followed was a mockery of justice. But then I had long since learned to expect no justice from the law.

Foremost among the inequities was that the presiding justice was Ronald Sepin, the same man with whom I had quarreled so long before, after the unfortunate death of Texas cattleman Ellis Runkel. So long before.

There was, of course, no way I could introduce this information as reason for a change of venue, and my attorneys, provided for me by friends in Denver, were often mystified by the grossly unfair rulings that spewed from the bench of supposed justice.

Dore recovered from his wounds sufficiently to testify in court from a hospital litter—itself a blatantly unfair influencing of the jury—and told a series of lies, claiming that I had threatened to kill him if he did not agree to the business propositions of my employers.

It has already been shown that this testimony was wholly false. And I had no employers at the time.

The prosecutor, a man in league with Judge Sepin, showed that Dore's partners in the Lady M mine had already signed options for the sale of all owned shares in the property and that they were to be the inheritors of Burton

Dore's shares in the event of his death, thus extending the options already in hand to full ownership of the property if Dore were to die. Of this I had no knowledge—nor interest—yet it was used as a circumstantial tool to defame me.

My plea to the charges lodged against me—murder and attempted murder—was a straightforward and time-honored matter of defense of my person against assault and possible death.

In any other court in the land this defense and the true facts as I have related them here would have been more than sufficient to secure my release. Before Ronald Sepin, however, my defense counsel was time and again thwarted in his efforts on my behalf, while the prosecutor was encouraged to paint as black a picture of me as possible. I was depicted to the jury as a killer and a gunman rather than the free enterprise entrepreneur I really am, and the existence of ancient wants and warrants against me—however falsely placed—was allowed to come to the attention of the jurors.

It became obvious that Ronald Sepin would accept no verdict save that of "guilty," and so it was no great surprise when the foreman read the words and Sepin had the obvious pleasure of sentencing me to hang by the neck until dead.

This sentence will, of course, not hold up under appeal, and I am now marshalling my forces toward that end. My Denver attorneys are already vigorously engaged in appeal proceedings, and I have written to my old and dear friends with the railroad, seeking their assistance as well.

It is my fond hope that once these true facts are known—as opposed to the scurrilous accounts presented by sensation-seeking journalists—I not only will again be a free man but will then be enabled to rejoin my dear wife Cynthia and spend the rest of my days in her gracious company.

In the meantime I am made comfortable in my confinement by the respectful company of those who wish to visit with the legendary Jason Evers. And if some of them are merely hangers-on who wish to see a legend defanged and helpless, the majority are my true friends and can be counted on to the end, however distant that may be.

I have, too, the comforting knowledge that I am and ever was an honorable man, that I acted only in the right, and that the day will come again when I can ride free and head high with the good .44 in my waistband and a stout horse between my knees.

To all of this I do swear and attest.

[s] Jason Evers
Manitou Springs, Colorado
January 11, 1879

# Epilogue

Jason Randolph Evers, b. Oct. 29, 1849, was hanged to death under my supervision, as directed by the Circuit Court, on the twelfth day of June, 1879, at El Paso County, Colorado, following due process of law and after exhausting all legal remedies and appeal procedures.

This manuscript was found among his personal possessions following his death by hanging. I have taken the liberty of reading it, but must reluctantly demur from commenting on the inaccuracies contained herein. However, having gone that far I might note that the inaccuracies I refer to are ones of motive and method and do not contest the facts of his many killings. If anything, those facts are represented on the short end of the scale.

The document was offered as memorabilia to Mrs. Cynthia Mische Jackson of Lincoln, N.M., as she was listed by the subject as sole surviving kin. No response was obtained.

I therefore submit the manuscript to the custody of the County Clerk, El Paso County, Colorado, for safekeeping until or unless it may be claimed by surviving members of the Evers family.

[s] Honus R. Crandall, SHERIFF
Colorado Springs, Colorado
September 22, 1879

# *Hayseed*

# FRANK RODERUS

Arnie Rasmussen is a big guy, with the general build of a young ox, and he might not know much, but he knows one thing: He loves Katherine Mulraney. Sure, she's too good for him; she is beautiful and fine, and he is, well, just Arnie. Just as he is steeling his nerve to talk to her, she disappears. Folks say she up and ran off with a fancy travelling man, but Arnie can't believe that. So he sets off after her. But the Wyoming Territory is a mighty tough place, and Arnie has never been off of his father's ranch. He has a lot to learn, and he'll learn all right . . . the hard way.

___4432-1                                                     $4.50 US/$5.50 CAN

# Old Marsden

# FRANK RODERUS

When he was born his parents named him Alvin, but that was a good long time ago. These days pretty much everybody just calls him Cap. Maybe he isn't quite as spry as he was back in his trapping days, but he can still sit a horse and his aim is almost as fine as ever. Most of the time, though, he is perfectly content to regale his granddaughter with tales of his exploits. But when someone kidnaps that lovely little girl, Cap isn't about to leave her rescue up to somebody else. He won't rest until she is home safe and sound—and until whoever took her learns just how much grit Cap still has in him.

___4506-0                                    $4.50 US/$5.50 CAN

# THE ACTOR

## ROBERT J. CONLEY

Bluford Steele had always been an outsider until he found his calling as an actor. Instead of being just another half-breed Cherokee with a white man's education, he can be whomever he chooses. But when the traveling acting troupe he is with arrives in the wild, lawless town of West Riddle, the man who rules the town with an iron fist forces them to perform. Then he steals all the proceeds. Steele is determined to get the money back, even if it means playing the most dangerous role of his life—a cold-blooded gunslinger ready to face down any man who gets in his way.

___4498-6                                          $4.50 US/$5.50 CAN

# THE HUNTING OF TOM HORN

Lively, action-packed, exciting, this is a collection of short masterpieces by one of the West's greatest storytellers. The characters in these tales—be they cowboy or bounty hunter, preacher or killer—are living, breathing people, people whose stories could be told only by a master like Will Henry.

___4484-6                                    $5.50 US/$6.50 CAN